Letters From Grace

Letters From Grace

C.J. Carmichael

TULE
PUBLISHING

Dedication

Dedicated to my beloved new granddaughter
Madeleine Kay Binnion Klein

Acknowledgments

I'm so grateful to be able to work with Jane Porter and the exceptional team at Tule Publishing.

For this book I want to single out the contribution by my editor Sinclair Sawhney. Getting a revision letter from Sinclair is like hearing from your most enthusiastic fan and your most astute, yet kind, critic. Thanks, Sinclair, for all your insights on making *Letters From Grace* a better story.

September 2, 1999
New York University

Dear Levi,

Here it is—my first letter to you. Which feels crazy since we text all the time. But there is something nice about actually writing your thoughts on paper.

I'm in New York City! I have to keep telling myself this because I can hardly believe it. I only wish I'd been able to convince you to come with me. You would love it! Have all the girls at UVM fallen for you yet? It's okay if they have, as long as you don't fall for them.

My roommate is friendly, maybe too friendly. Our room is becoming party central. I have to go to the library if I want any peace. That's where I am now...thinking of you.

Chapter One

Woodland, New York, September 2019

A s JESSICA SHANAHAN pulled her father's old college yearbooks from a storage container in their attic, she noticed a shoebox amid the rest of his college memorabilia. On the lid in neat round letters—her father's script when he was printing—was the word "Grace."

Jessica set aside the pile of yearbooks and lifted the lid. Inside was a stack of letters addressed to her father at his former residence hall at the University of Vermont. As she flipped through the letters, she saw that all the letters— except the final one—were from the same person: Grace Hamilton.

When Jessica was only two her mother, Maggie, was killed in a car accident. Her dad had often told her the story of meeting her mom in his first year of college, how it had been love at first sight, and that he considered himself the luckiest of men when he asked Maggie Brown to marry him and she told him yes.

He always made it sound like her mother had been the one and only love of his life.

And yet he'd kept this box of old letters from another woman.

"Are they up there?"

Jessica's best friend, Max Stedwell, was downstairs holding the ladder. Like her, Max had applied to the University of Vermont—though it wasn't his first choice—and was interested in seeing her dad's old yearbooks.

"Um…yeah." She grabbed the books and handed them down to Max. She hesitated over the shoebox. The letters were addressed to her dad, so technically off-limits. But they were so old, he couldn't really care, could he? Besides, he'd already given her permission to look through his old college stuff.

She tucked the shoebox under her arm and started down the ladder.

Max peered up at her. "What's in the box?"

"Old letters." She rested the box on one of the rungs of the ladder as she fitted the attic cover back into place. Then she scrambled the rest of the way down. "I'm going to check them out later."

She ducked into her room where she tucked the box under her chemistry textbook before joining Max in the family room. He was already sprawled on the sectional, leafing through one of the yearbooks. She flopped down next to him, leaning over his shoulder so she could see too.

"Is your dad happy you've decided to go to good old UVM?"

"He doesn't care that much, as long as I go somewhere." Jessica didn't know why her dad was so obsessed with college. If she was going to take over the family general store, why bother? She'd been learning on the job since she was four years old. A business degree wasn't going to change anything.

"I wish my folks had the same attitude. They want me as close to home as possible."

Max's dream was to study geology at the University of Colorado. Selfishly Jess wished he'd stay closer to home, too.

"Dad keeps going on about how college is so much fun and opens so many doors."

"I like the story he told us the other night about meeting your mother in the campus library," Max said. "The spider coming down from the ceiling and landing in her hair…and how he heard her scream and came to her rescue."

"Yeah, and bravely scooped the spider into his hands and took it outside." Jess rolled her eyes. She might mock her father a little from time to time, but mostly they got along really well.

"Since your dad is so cool, maybe he'd let you come to Colorado with me?" Max gave her his best, beseeching smile.

For many years Max's smile was something Jess took for granted. But lately it had been having a potent effect on her. Especially when he looked directly at her with that mischievous sparkle in his eyes.

The way he was now.

She knew Max liked her. They'd been friends forever. But did he "like" her? When he smiled at her this way it seemed impossible that he didn't. But even though she leaned a fraction closer to him, he did not take the next step and reach for her hand. Or kiss her.

"Colorado's too far."

"For you or your dad?"

"Me," she admitted.

"You are such a homebody," Max teased. "Maybe I should change my mind and go to Vermont, too. It would be cheaper. I don't want to be drowning in debt when I graduate."

Jess knew what he meant. All their friends were stressed about how to finance their degrees. Not many had folks who could afford to cover the entire cost. Jess was lucky her dad had started a savings account for her when she was a baby. When she'd started working at his general store officially, as a teenager, he'd insisted she deposit fifty percent of each paycheck into that account.

Of course she was also lucky her dad owned the store and so she had a guaranteed job for as little or as much spare time as she had available. Max wasn't so fortunate. His father worked at a plastics factory and his mom at a local grocery store—neither one could offer him work on a schedule tailor-made for him. Last summer, when Max couldn't find a job, he'd started his own dog-walking business. That had been cool—most of the dogs were adorable—but he hadn't made even half of what she had earned at the store.

"Hopefully you'll get a good job this summer," Jess said.

"Yeah. Maybe."

While Jess didn't have the same financial challenges as Max, she did have her own concerns about college—in particular, leaving her father. Max's parents had each other and their twin daughters, five years younger than Max. Her dad had no one.

In all the years since Jess's mom had died, he'd dated only sporadically, and never seriously. He went out of his way to keep her mother's memory alive—for her benefit Jess thought—which was sweet in a way, but maybe not so healthy for him. For too long his life had been all about raising Jess, working at the family general store and Sunday dinners with her grandparents. He needed to expand his horizons.

Max looked up from the yearbook. "I'm hungry."

"You're always hungry. There's some apples in the kitchen. Grab me one while you're at it."

When Max returned he stretched out his legs onto the old pine coffee table, next to hers. After his first bite he said, "Looks like the birds are hungry too."

Jess glanced through the window to the gnarly red oak tree that had supported Jess's tire swing when she was little and from which now hung one of the multiple bird feeders her father kept stocked in the yard.

Several house finches were currently jockeying for position so they could feed on the seed and nut mixture. Though Jess wasn't as crazy about birds as her father was, she did enjoy watching their antics.

Max focused back on the yearbook. After a few minutes he said, "Look, here's your dad." He pointed at one square in a sea of faces.

"Huh." Given that her dad's hobbies were playing chess and ornithology she'd expected his college photo to be dorky. But he actually looked good. Broad shoulders, friendly eyes, a confident smile.

"Hasn't changed much, has he?" Max said.

"Really?" She studied the photo more closely. Max was right. Why had she never noticed how good-looking her dad was? She found her mother's photo next.

Max whistled. "Wow. That could almost be you."

"Except for the nerdy hair and glasses." But she was secretly pleased Max thought she looked like her pretty mother.

As Max continued to flip pages, Jess tried to tune out the fluttering awareness she felt at being so close to him. The campus with its historic red buildings really was beautiful, but she got a car-sick queasy feeling when she tried to insert herself into the picture. Which was so lame. All her life she'd been excited for the day when she would be one of the senior girls at high school. But now that it was finally her turn, anxiety about the future was taking all the fun out of it.

She tried to put her feelings into words. "The thing

about being in our last year of school, is that nothing has changed, yet nothing feels the same."

"Yeah, it's weird. The last time for so many things," Max said.

"Exactly. Our last year at Woodland High. Last year on cross-country and the track team. Probably the last year we'll live full-time with our parents."

"Basically our last year of avoiding adulthood."

In that moment Jess felt that no one would ever understand her the way Max did. Their connection went back all the way to kindergarten and a mutual love of Legos. Their interests had evolved as they grew older. There was the year they were obsessed with the Harry Potter books and movies, the multiple years they were crazed about Fortnite, and—most recently—their love of long-distance running. Recently they'd made a pact that they would run their first marathon together this spring. Already Max had made a training schedule for them.

She and Max had a wider circle of friends that they hung out with on weekends. Most of them assumed they were a romantic couple. When she and Max were fifteen, she'd thought they were headed in that direction, but then Max had asked pretty, redheaded Hannah to go to a school dance with him. They'd only dated a few months—and Max had still made time for Jess as a friend—but it had been a clear signal to Jess that she would only ever be a buddy to Max.

So she'd tried a bit of dating, too. But it felt weird to her.

Most of her girlfriends had had at least one serious relationship by now. She didn't know what was wrong with her. Was she just an extremely late bloomer?

She glanced at Max, following the line of his long legs to the coffee table where his bare foot was just inches from hers. She imagined shifting her foot, touching her toes to his, and felt a delicious tingle all over her body.

No, she'd definitely bloomed. Unfortunately, the only guy she cared about hadn't noticed.

LEVI SHANAHAN GENERALLY enjoyed the walk home from work. His route took him down Main Street, past the library and the elementary school, then finally to Lincoln Avenue. Here the sugar maples grew so tall and full that their branches arched over his head. Today the red tinge of the leaves told him, better than a calendar, that autumn was finally here. He could see the evidence, too, in the front yards of his neighbors as he walked by. Formerly lush flowers in front gardens and pots had grown leggy and were beginning to brown.

Autumn was a beautiful time in Woodland. But this year he welcomed the season with mixed emotions. This was the last fall he'd have Jessica home with him. A year from now he'd be heading for an empty house. Levi didn't know how he was going to manage. He hadn't expected to still feel so young at this point in his life. But then, he'd only been twenty when Jess was born. Only two years older than she was right now.

Crazy.

He liked Jessica's friend—boyfriend?—Max a lot. But he hoped Jess was at least in her mid-twenties before she thought of marriage.

Baskets of yellow and orange chrysanthemums and half a dozen pumpkins welcomed him on the small front porch when he reached his home. It wasn't just to advertise his store's products that he made this effort. As a widowed father he'd always done his best to make a warm, cozy home for his daughter. He knew little touches made a big difference. And it was all worth the effort when he saw Jessica smile.

As he reached for the front door, he almost collided with Max.

"Hey, Mr. S."

"Max." He stepped aside so the teenager—now, at six feet, the same height as Levi—could pass. "Want to stay for dinner?" He'd brought a chicken potpie home from the store, and there would be plenty.

"Thanks but Mom and Dad want me home tonight. We're having some sort of family meeting."

"Big news, you think?"

"Last time it was to tell us we needed to do more chores around the house. So probably not." Max gave a casual salute, then leapt over the three porch steps before breaking into a nice, easy lope. Max would probably run all the way home. Levi wished he still had that kind of energy.

In a way he was glad Max wasn't staying for dinner tonight. He'd reached the point where he was cherishing every hour he got to spend alone with his daughter. Between her friends, track, and the time she spent studying, it felt like he was lucky to get thirty minutes in a day.

Inside he found his daughter in the kitchen, making a salad as he'd asked her to do in a text just before leaving work. Her pretty, honey-colored hair was gathered in a messy bun and she was chopping a cucumber.

"Hey, kid." He kissed her forehead when she turned to give him a smile. "Have a good day?"

"We checked out those yearbooks like you suggested. Found your and Mom's grad photos. Max thought Mom looked a lot like me."

"Two prettiest women ever."

"You were kind of a hottie back then, too, Dad. What happened?"

"Smart-ass." He set the shopping bag on the counter. "I'm going to change. Be right back."

Once he was in his old jeans and a clean black T-shirt, he washed his face and hands in the small en suite. When he returned to the kitchen he asked, "So what did you think of the yearbooks? Besides checking out the old photos of your parents."

"Kind of inspiring."

He was glad to hear that. "It's a great school. Not that I expect you to go there just because I did."

"I know, Dad."

He wanted her to feel free to pursue whatever career or life she wanted. Still, he couldn't help being pleased that she'd chosen a college so close to home that he'd still see her on long weekends and holidays.

"Say, Dad, did you ever date anyone before Mom?"

He'd been pulling dishes from the cabinet. He set them down and turned to her. "Why do you ask?"

"Just wondering."

He tried sidestepping the question. "I met your mom just a few weeks after spring break. The rest is history."

"But what about before that? Like in high school?"

"There was this one girl. But she went to college in New York. We drifted apart." It was curious how a person could summarize one of the happiest and yet most painful experiences in their life with just three short sentences. He hoped his daughter would drop the subject now. "Are you going to make the salad dressing or should I?"

"I already made it. Tell me more about the girl?"

Levi hesitated. Then realized he was being foolish. After all these years it didn't matter. "She and her family moved to Woodland when I was in seventh grade. She was in my class and we became friends after working on a science project together. We stayed friends all through high school, sort of like you and Max."

"So you were just friends?"

Is that all she and Max were? For years Levi had been expecting his daughter to tell him the relationship had turned romantic, but as far as he knew it hadn't happened yet.

"Well. More than friends, I guess." Much more. Grace had been his first love as well as his best friend. She'd meant so much to him that it was hard to describe their relationship in words. Certainly not to his daughter.

"What was her name?"

"Grace Hamilton." Just saying her name made his heart contract. He couldn't believe it still had that much power.

"Have I ever met her?"

"No." He fixed his gaze out the kitchen window, at a hummingbird feeder that had been sitting empty for more than a month. He ought to wash it and put it away until next spring. "Her parents moved to Florida shortly after we started college and she's never been back to Woodland. At least not that I know of."

Jess put the salad on the table, between their two place settings. "Was she into bird watching and chess like you?"

"Grace is the one who taught me how to play chess. And yeah, she would come with me when I went birding. She was more into photographing them though."

"So she was just as nerdy as you?"

His daughter loved to tease him about his uncool hobbies. But he'd also played football and being part of the team had brought him acceptance and a measure of popularity. "Grace was too beautiful to be considered a nerd."

His daughter shot him one of those looks that laid him bare. "Did she break your heart, Dad?"

He swallowed. "That was a long time ago."

A chirp from his phone distracted the both of them. He took a quick glance at the screen and frowned. "It's the mayor. She's reminding me about the festival meeting tomorrow night." Erin Powers was also suggesting they grab dinner together beforehand. He quickly tapped back his reply. *Good for the meeting but having dinner with Jess.*

"She likes you. Why don't you ask her for dinner before the meeting?"

"What are you, a mind reader? That's what Erin suggested. But I'd rather eat at home with you."

"I'm going to college next year. What are you going to do then? Eat all your meals alone?"

"You're not in college yet. And you shouldn't worry about me. I've got lots of friends. And Grandma and Grandpa." His parents lived just a mile away and Sunday dinner was a long-standing tradition.

"So that's it? You're not even forty and you plan to spend all your weekends with your parents?"

Was that what this interest in his ex-girlfriends had been about? "Erin Powers is pretty and smart...but she's not my type. And for the record I can handle my own love life, thanks."

"You'd need to have a love life to handle it, Dad."

Levi hated to admit it. But his daughter had a point.

That same evening…Sparks Book Store, Manhattan

PHOTOJOURNALIST GRACE HAMILTON smiled at the gentleman who had just asked her to sign four copies of her newest book, *National Park Birds and Their Stories.* He was planning to give them to his adult children for Christmas and she had individually inscribed each book.

"I hope they enjoy them, Mr. Bronson."

"I'm sure they will. We're real nature lovers in our family. And I've always loved your work for Audubon."

Grace didn't try to rush the chatty gentleman, even though people were lined up through the front door and down Broadway for two whole blocks. This intel came from her agent, Jeremy Browne, who was currently chatting with her editor at Dover Books: Paula Baton. They looked pleased with the turnout. Grace was thrilled.

The book was the culmination of a five-year project for her. She'd traveled to every national park in the country, woken before dawn and the morning chorus to get the best photos, and stayed up late doing post-production in rustic lodges where guests were required to share bathrooms and forget about cell service or cable TV.

Not that Grace minded the lack of amenities. She was

too focused on her work and she would have been happy to camp, except for the need to charge batteries and download her photographs to her laptop.

The next person to step up to her table was a woman, dressed in a smart camel trench coat over a black, silk jumpsuit. Grace lifted her gaze to the woman's face, and then jumped out of her chair.

"Alicia!" She reached over the table to embrace her best friend from Woodland—the small town in upper New York State where Grace had lived for a time with her parents. She and Alicia Moretti kept in touch via texts and video chats, but between Grace's travel schedule and Alicia's responsibilities to her husband, children and yoga studio, they only managed to meet in person about once a year, always in Manhattan.

A few times Grace had offered to meet her friend in Woodland, but Alicia wouldn't hear of it. While she loved raising a family in a small town, Alicia looked forward to her annual trip to the city and indulging in fine dining, theater and shopping.

Besides, there really was no reason for Grace to go back to Woodland since her parents didn't live there anymore. This way, too, Grace could avoid the possibility of running into Levi Shanahan and being reminded of her biggest regret. When she was eighteen, she'd thought there'd be lots of guys she'd fall in love with the way she'd loved Levi. In actual fact there'd been none.

Alicia knew about her conflicted feelings for Levi, but by mutual accord they didn't speak about him very often. Occasionally Alicia injected news of Levi into their conversations, but she always did so casually. That was how Grace had learned of Levi's marriage, the birth of his daughter, and then just two years later, his wife's tragic death. Grace had sent a signed book for the wedding—which she hadn't been invited to—and flowers for Maggie's funeral and had received a polite thank-you note for both. That was the only correspondence she and Levi had had in about twenty years.

"I wanted to surprise you," Alicia said. "And it looks like I have."

Grace laughed. "I'll say. You look marvelous by the way. When did you get here?"

"Around noon. I've already done some shopping. Isn't this a sweet jumpsuit?" Alicia glanced behind her. "But I shouldn't hold you up. So many people are waiting. You done good, girl." She gave her friend a quick hug.

"We'll have lots of time to visit later, right? You are staying a few nights, aren't you?" All her friend was carrying were some shopping bags and a stylish purse. "Where is your luggage?"

"Locked up at Penn Station."

"Great. We'll pick it up on our way home after the reception. Red wine and artisanal cheeses and schmoozing with the literary and ornithological crowd..." Grace, who had never mastered the art of small talk with strangers and working a room, was not looking forward to it. "Sorry, but there's no way to avoid it."

"Why would I want to? Sounds like fun. Is Harvey here?"

"Yes. He'll be thrilled to see you." Harvey Peters was both her landlord and closest friend in Manhattan and Alicia loved hearing stories from his former career as a set designer on Broadway.

"Oh good." Alicia squeezed her shoulder. "You have the most glamorous life!"

"Hardly." But Alicia had already moved on and didn't hear her. Since Alicia only visited when she was in Manhattan, she didn't realize how she spent the majority of her time. Pre-dawn wake-up calls, followed by miles of trudging through forests, marshes and tidal pools. Hours spent waiting in dirty, damp, cold locations hoping to catch the perfect bird in the perfect moment, and then, after a hurried shower and dinner, her nights were not spent reading or binge-watching shows, but at the computer doing post-production work.

It wasn't a life many could tolerate. But Grace loved it. All except for the part where she fell into bed exhausted— and alone.

Well. Not always alone. Grace had met a lot of attractive and eligible men during her years as a freelance photojournalist and she'd had relationships with a few. But conflicting schedules eventually led to a parting of the ways. Or at least they had so far. Grace hadn't given up on finding a partner to share her life with. But if she didn't, she would be okay. That's what she kept telling herself. And mostly she believed it.

September 5, 1999
New York University

Dear Levi,

Got up early today to do some birding in Central Park. (My roommate wasn't in her bed. Guess she crashed at some party last night. She's still pissed at me for turning the lights out on her and her friends last week at midnight. But it was a Monday, for Gods sake, and my Tuesday schedule is insane.) Anyway, Central Park. It was crazy, a warbler storm of Cape Mays and Tennessees and black-throated greens. Someday Im going to make a book about the birds that migrate through this park—and you're going to help me. I miss you so much...

Chapter Two

"IRV, I RECOMMEND the combination snow shovel." Levi handed the elderly man his best-selling shovel. "It's good for pushing and shoveling snow. The steel blade will scrape snow down to bare concrete, while the polypropylene blade makes it lighter to lift."

Irvine Mackenzie studied the new shovel suspiciously. Levi had been running through the pros and cons of his various snow shovels for the past fifteen minutes. He knew that once Irvine made up his mind on what he wanted he would head home to his computer to find a better price online.

That was the way things went in the retail business these days. Levi didn't mind so much in Irvine's case because his wife, Sondra, met her friends at his lunch counter five days a week.

But today Irvine shocked him by handing over the combination snow shovel.

"I'll take it."

Levi could hardly hide his surprise. "Great. I'll ring it up for you."

"I could get it cheaper at a big box store," Irv grumbled. "But Sondra says we have to support our local retailers, or they'll go out of business."

Levi paused. "If you want to try and find a better price…"

"No, no, this is good."

Levi was carrying the shovel out to Irvine's car when Erin Powers waved at him from across the street. He waved back then popped the shovel into Irvine's trunk. "Now you're ready for that first snow fall. Hopefully it won't be coming for at least a month."

"Not until after the Autumn Foliage Festival anyway," Irv said. "Sondra's going to be selling her jams and cherry pies."

"Her pies are my favorite. Can't wait to stock up." Levi closed the trunk, then stepped back to the sidewalk as Irv drove away.

Erin waved at him again, then crossed the street. She was in her first term as town mayor and Levi figured the job might be hers in perpetuity if she wanted. Everyone in town loved her. She was incredibly positive and high-energy, and the first to volunteer when help was needed.

Her long-time boyfriend had recently taken a job in Boston and ended their relationship. Her recent invite to dinner had Levi suspecting Erin had identified him as a potential replacement. He hoped someone else would come along to catch her eye. While he admired Erin a lot, too much time in her company exhausted him.

"Hey, Erin."

"Levi."

She looked attractive in a long butterscotch-colored sweater, jeans and tan boots. The colors suited her red hair and hazel eyes. Thinking of his daughter's comment last night, about him needing a social life, Levi waited to feel a stir of attraction, of connection. It didn't come.

"Isn't it a beautiful day?" she enthused. "So exciting watching the leaves start to turn. Knowing that every day is going to be more glorious than the one before until we reach peak autumn foliage colors. Don't you just love going for long drives in the country this time of year?"

"I prefer hiking." Autumn was a great season for birders and this year's southern migration was already in full swing. "Last Sunday in the Bruce Preserve I saw close to a hundred broad-winged hawks."

"Hawks. Hm. That's interesting." Her quizzical frown suggested the opposite, but that didn't stop her from tipping her head to one side and giving him a brilliant smile. "Were you out with a group?"

"Nope." Though he was generally a social guy, he preferred to do his birding alone with few exceptions, one of which was his daughter. Some of his fondest memories were of the days they'd spent outdoors together, Jess working her way through one of the scavenger hunts he'd organized for her, while he trained his binoculars on interesting birds.

Sometimes he'd take a sketch pad along and make drawings. But he didn't often have time for that.

"Well, if you're ever looking for company, give me a call. I love to hike."

"Right." Levi doubted his idea of a hike in nature would be the same as Erin's. "I'll keep that in mind." He glanced back at his store. "I ought to get back to work. See you later tonight?"

"I'm looking forward to it." Erin gave him another of her big smiles before heading toward her office where she worked as a real estate agent. A town the size of Woodland didn't have the tax base, or the need, for a full-time mayor.

Levi had almost made it inside his store when another familiar voice called out his name. His mother. He turned to see her familiar rotund figure approaching from the opposite direction of Erin's office. Familiar and yet not. When had her hair turned from salt and pepper to gray? And when had she developed that slope in her shoulders? He felt a pang of sadness at this evidence of aging.

"Hey, Mom. Meeting your friends for coffee?"

"Yes. I tried to convince your father to come, but I couldn't lure him away from the television."

They shared a worried glance. Since his diagnosis of atherosclerosis a month ago Pat Shanahan had been in a mild depression, despite being assured by his physician that with some healthy lifestyle changes—walking was good, heavy labor was not—and medication, the condition could be improved.

"I've got a meeting tonight," Levi said. "But I'll stop by to visit him tomorrow and see if I can convince him to come out for a walk."

"Thanks, son. By the way, I saw you chatting up our mayor. Wasn't she looking pretty?"

Levi groaned. First his daughter, now his mother. "Is there some sort of matchmaking conspiracy between you and Jess?"

"Maybe." Mischief danced in his mother's blue eyes. "Sometimes I think you forget how young you are, son. Since Maggie died you've been focused on your daughter and that's been admirable. But Jess will be off to college soon."

"No need to remind me of that." He thought about it all the time already.

"So. Don't you think it's time you focused on your own needs now?"

"I've got all I need. Family, friends and a good job."

"But what about someone to keep you company in the evenings? Someone special to love?"

"I have been thinking about that," he admitted. "And I've decided that after I drop Jess off at college I'm going to adopt a dog."

His mother laughed, then shook her head. "You're incorrigible."

He walked his mom to the back of the store where her

friends were waiting at the lunch counter for Connie Wilson—an old high school friend he'd hired when she'd needed a job after her divorce—to serve them.

"You have to admit," he told his mother, "a dog ticks all the boxes."

His mother raised her eyebrows. "Not *all* the boxes."

That was true. A sex life would be nice. Definitely. But he wasn't into casual relationships and when it came to true, head-over-heels love, he'd already struck gold twice. First Grace. Then Maggie.

He was open to it happening again. But he wasn't holding out a lot of hope.

"REMEMBER THAT SHOEBOX I found in the attic yesterday?" Jess and Max had just finished a five-mile training run and were heading toward Jess's house. Usually they chatted a lot after their runs. But today Max kept grabbing quick looks at his phone, then stuffing it back into his pocket.

"Yeah."

He didn't sound at all interested, but Jess persevered. "It was full of love letters from Dad's old high school sweetheart. They broke up when she moved to New York to study photography."

"You didn't read them?"

Jess's face, already glowing from exertion, heated up a

few more degrees. She'd been so curious she hadn't been able to stop herself. But yeah, she knew it was wrong. "Well, a few of them…"

Max shot her a look that was definitely unimpressed. "How would you feel if he cyber-snooped you on Instagram?"

"I'd be pissed. Yeah. But the point is, when I asked him if he had a girlfriend before Mom, you should have seen his face. I think he really loved this girl."

"So?"

"So, I'm going to college next year. And he's going to be alone. He doesn't seem interested in any of the single women in town—not even Erin Powers and you have to admit she's kind of beautiful."

"She's okay." Without breaking stride, Max took a swig from his water bottle.

"So I started wondering about this girl from high school. And I googled her. And guess what I discovered?"

"That it's none of your business?"

"Damn it, Max. Why are you being such a grouch today?"

He slowed his pace for a fraction and looked like he was considering telling her something important. But all he said was, "Sorry. What did you find?"

"Grace Hamilton is actually a pretty famous photojournalist. She lives in Manhattan and she just published a book of her photographs and stories about birds in the national parks."

They were at her house now. Jess took a key from her pocket and unlocked the front door. First she went to the fruit basket on the counter to grab a couple bananas. She and Max both craved bananas after a long run.

"Thanks." Max peeled it open and ate almost half of it in one bite. "Did you say Grace Hamilton? You have one of her books on your coffee table don't you?"

She looked at her friend, impressed, then went to the family room to pick up a book that had been part of the home décor for so long it had become invisible to her. Sure enough, under the title, *Birds of Central Park*, was the name Grace Hamilton.

"Huh. I had no idea. Dad never mentioned he knew the photographer." She opened the book to the title page. *Congratulations, Maggie and Levi. Wishing you every happiness.*

"Looks like it was a wedding gift to my parents." Had her mother felt weird getting a gift from her husband's ex-girlfriend? Jess had enough evidence—old photos and videos and stories from her dad—to know that her parents had been very happy together. So probably her mom had shrugged it off.

Max leaned close to her as she flipped through the pages. The photographs were stunning. But Jess was far more aware of the warmth emanating from Max's body. So close. If only he would slip an arm around her shoulders. Maybe then…

But instead of touching Jess, Max pulled out his phone. Soon he'd found Grace Hamilton's website.

"Looks like her latest book made the *New York Times* bestseller list," Max said. "Impressive."

Jess already knew this. "Check the 'About the Author' tab. According to her bio she lives in Manhattan. No mention of a husband or kids."

Max shook his head. "I can guess what you're thinking. Don't go there."

"Why not? Dad doesn't seem interested in the mayor. Maybe I'd have more luck fixing him up with his old girlfriend."

"You don't think it's a problem they don't live in the same city?"

"She's a photographer. She can live anywhere. I'm going to send her an email." Jess snatched her phone back and began typing.

"You've got to be kidding me..." Max shifted closer, again, so he could see her phone.

Jess had opened the "Contact Me" page of Grace Hamilton's website and now she began typing. She'd been thinking about this all day so the words came easily.

Dear Ms. Hamilton,

I'm a senior at Woodland High, working on a project about women in successful careers. Since you grew up in Woodland, too, I thought you would make the perfect subject for my paper. If you could spare an hour or so I'd love to interview you about how you became a photojournalist and about any challenges you faced in your career as a woman. Since the project is supposed to include visuals I'd really love to get a photo of us together so I get extra points for meeting you in person. I can drive to Poughkeepsie and take the train to Penn Station. Maybe we could meet at a coffee shop near there? Thank you for considering my request. I look forward to meeting you!

Sincerely, Rae Stedwell

Before Max had a chance to comment, she hit "Send."

"Hey! You used my last name."

And she'd used her second name, not her first. "I don't want her to know I'm Levi's daughter." Even as she spoke the words, Jessica saw how shortsighted her plan was. Max was quick to point out the error in her thinking.

"If you do get her to hook up with your dad, don't you think she's going to find out who you really are?" Max tilted his head back and pulled on his hair with both hands, a sure sign he was frustrated. "And what if she googles Rae Stedwell the way you googled her and finds out Rae doesn't exist?"

"Not everyone uses their real name on social media. She won't think much about it. And if my plan works and they get together, they'll be too happy to be mad at me."

"It's quite a leap from interviewing her in Manhattan, to getting her to see your father again."

"I have that figured out. I'm going to try to convince her

30

to come to the Woodland Autumn Foliage Festival. She can rent a tent to display her photographs. As a local girl who's done well, she'll be a big hit."

"Our little festival won't attract someone at her level." Max was still looking at her like she was crazy.

"Why not? It'll give her an excuse to visit her hometown. I'm sure she has friends and maybe even some family she'd like to visit."

"And why did you put in that bit about wanting a photo with her? You sound like a stalker."

"I need an excuse to meet in person. I'm not setting her up with my dad until I check her out." Jess was talking too fast. She always did that when she was nervous. Why hadn't she at least read over her message a few times before hitting send? She wasn't usually this impulsive.

Max held out his phone so she could see Grace's photo posted beside her bio. "Look at this woman. Does she look like she would fit in here in Woodland?"

Jess looked. Grace had sleek, shoulder-length blond hair and round blue eyes. Her clothing and the way she held her body gave the impression of relaxed elegance. She did not, Jess had to admit, look like someone who would want to be the wife of a man who owned a small-town general store.

"Oh man. I'm such a dweeb. You're right, she's way out of my dad's league." She took a deep breath. "Oh well. I bet she doesn't even answer my message."

"Probably not," Max agreed.

"Then let's stop talking about her and start studying for our chem exam."

"Agreed." Max went to retrieve his backpack, which he'd left on the front porch before they went for their run. He'd no sooner pulled out his study notes than a chime sounded on Jess's phone. She glanced at her screen.

"Holy crap, Max. She's answered me already." Jess's fingers froze over the icon that would open the email.

"Well...?"

At his prompting she finally tapped her screen and then scanned Grace Hamilton's reply. "Oh man, what have I done?"

With a grunt of impatience, Max grabbed her phone so he could read for himself. When he was finished, he shook his head. "She's invited you this Saturday! What are you going to do?"

"I guess I'm going to go."

"What will you tell your dad?"

"The truth. Well...part of the truth. I'll say we're going to Manhattan for the day to do some research for a school project."

"How is that truthful? You do remember you invented the school project?"

Jess had been thinking about that and thought she'd found a solution. "My English lit teacher wants a book report every month. I'll ask him if I can do my September one on Grace Hamilton's new book. If I tell him I've set up an interview with the actual photographer I bet he'll say yes."

Max studied her face for several seconds. "Maybe. But what about your dad? You think he'll let you go to Manhattan alone?"

"Not likely. Which is why you're coming with me."

"Hard pass."

Jess tugged on his arm. "Aw, don't be that way. We'll have fun, I promise. After the interview we can do touristy stuff like go to the top of the Empire State Building and run across the Brooklyn Bridge. And I'll pay for our train tickets."

"That part sounds cool. But meeting Grace Hamilton is like the worst idea ever."

She sat and stared at him, knowing he would break. Finally he heaved a big sigh.

"Fine. I'll come."

"Thanks, Max. Now...time to study?"

He shook his head. "It's getting late. Think I'll head home."

His comment reminded her why he'd left early yesterday. "How did the family meeting go? Did your parents have anything important to tell you?"

Max's face went blank. Then he blinked and shrugged. "Nothing important."

"Really?"

He shrugged again and she followed him to the kitchen where he tossed his banana peel into the compost container.

"See you tomorrow."

She watched out the window as he headed down the sidewalk. Something was different with him; something was off. Maybe he was annoyed she'd roped him into that trip to New York. She was kind of nervous about the trip, too, about the whole sketchy plan to interview her father's ex-girlfriend.

But that look on her father's face last night. She'd never forget it. Sort of wistful and sad and full of longing. And the way he'd said her name, *Grace Hamilton*, as if it had some sort of power over him.

She'd never seen her dad talk that way about any other woman—not even her mom.

Her dad had done so much for her. If she could help him find happiness, help him find love, then she wasn't going to let a little nervousness stop her from doing it.

September 7, 1999
New York University

Dear Levi,

Connie tells me you're having fun, meeting lots of people. That's so like you. I always wonder what you see in an introvert like me. My roommate has given up on me. She only comes to our room to sleep or change clothes and hardly talks to me anymore. Which is good, I guess, because I want to focus on my classes and now our room is almost always really quiet.

Chapter Three

"YOUR GRANDMA CAME into the store today," Levi told his daughter as they chopped vegetables for a tofu stir-fry. Last year Jess had convinced him they should eat vegetarian three nights a week. He had to admit the new diet felt good. And he was even starting to like some of the meals, though tofu would never be his favorite.

"Yeah? How are she and Grandpa doing?"

"Grandpa sounds depressed. And Grandma was looking older. Soon that big house of theirs is going to be too much for them."

"Oh, but I love their house. I can't imagine them anywhere else."

"I know what you mean. But your grandfather's got to make some lifestyle changes. Walking is good, but heavy lifting, climbing ladders…he shouldn't do any of that." It felt to Levi that life was changing too fast. His daughter's imminent departure for college was one thing. His parents' aging was another. Why did both of these have to happen at the same time? He supposed that was what they meant by the sandwich generation. He was now, officially, the tuna salad.

"I guess they could hire someone to do the yard work."

"Yeah. Or I could help them."

"Dad, you don't have to take care of everyone."

Levi tousled her hair, something she hated. It was sweet how she worried about him. He melted a teaspoon of coconut oil in the large frying pan, then added the onions. Once the onions were golden, Jess added the tofu, then the other vegetables.

"So how was your day?" he asked his daughter. "Did you and Max go for your run?"

"Yup. Five miles. He stopped in for a few minutes afterward, but he didn't stay long."

"I can't remember the last time he went two nights in a row without having dinner here," Levi noted, watching his daughter's face to see her reaction.

"Yeah. I'm not sure what's up with that."

Levi put the stir-fry and a bowl of rice on the table. As they sat down to eat he asked, "You two haven't had a disagreement or anything?"

"Nope. In fact we were thinking of taking the train to Manhattan on Saturday. I've got some research to do for a book report. And then we thought we'd have a little fun, play at being tourists for a few hours."

The request surprised Levi. He set down his fork and considered the idea. He could tell Jess was anxious as she watched him. He took a drink of water, then gave a nod.

"Sounds like fun. Can you be home by eight?"

"Sure."

Aware that she was still staring at him, Levi paused his eating again. "What's wrong?"

"I just thought this would be a bigger issue for you. That you would give me a list of do's and don'ts."

He'd been tempted to do just that. That's why he'd paused before he'd answered. He'd needed to give the idea some thought.

"By this point, Jess, I guess I've taught you all the do's and don'ts. You've demonstrated responsibility at school and working at the store. Next year you'll be on your own in college. I figure it's probably good for you to start spreading your wings a little."

"Cool."

"It has nothing to do with being cool. I'm letting you go because I trust you." He looked his daughter in the eyes the way he always did when he wanted to make sure she heard him. She didn't flinch, but she did swallow, which made him think she wasn't quite as brave as she was making out.

This was one of those moments when Levi felt the burden of being a single parent. It would be nice to talk decisions like this over with a spouse. Since he couldn't, he just had to hope he'd made the right call.

AN HOUR LATER at the festival meeting Levi zoned out as two of the committee members argued about something that didn't really matter. At least, not to him. Once upon a time, he'd been pretty passionate about the Autumn Foliage Festival. But he'd been on the committee for a lot of years now. He supposed he was getting burned out.

His mind drifted to the conversation he'd had with Jess yesterday. Funny that she would bring up his old girlfriend, when just that afternoon he'd gone online and ordered Grace's latest book. Back when they'd been high school sweethearts, Grace had told him she was going to be a famous photojournalist. And now she was.

He was glad for her. She had the magic combination: talent plus determination. Back when they were teenagers, she'd wanted him to be equally ambitious and she'd pleaded with him go to New York with her.

He'd been tempted, but practicality and finances had dictated he stay closer to home.

Grace had said it wouldn't matter. They could survive a long-distance romance.

But in the end—even though they stayed in touch with text messages and even old-fashioned snail mail—they hadn't lasted three months.

He'd kept all her letters, or so he'd thought. But last night, after Jess's questions, he'd gone looking for them and hadn't been able to find them. Maybe Maggie had thrown them out. Though it wasn't like her to do something like that without asking him first.

Right from their first meeting at the college library it was clear what a special person Maggie was. Kind and soft-hearted, but also funny and smart.

Once they were officially a couple, Levi resolved to put all his feelings for Grace aside. To forget about her, as best as he could. And he did it.

It wasn't just willpower. It was survival. Because a man couldn't keep living with the level of pain the end of that relationship had inflicted.

He'd only heard from Grace two times after their breakup. Once she'd sent a wedding gift for him and Maggie—which Maggie had written the thank-you letter for. And then three years later she'd sent him a flower arrangement and letter of condolence.

Since then he hadn't thought of her at all—well, hardly at all.

Levi tuned back in to the discussion.

Clara Quiver—who had been his civics teacher back in high school—currently had the floor. Since retirement she had put her civic-mindedness to full use. There was hardly a cause or a committee Clara would not volunteer for. In the case of the Autumn Foliage Festival, she was responsible for recruiting the artists to be featured in the festival.

"If we never try anything new our festival is going to get tired and eventually stop drawing crowds and—"

"Come on, Clara," argued Sam Rigby—former band director at Woodland High, and someone else who was a frequent volunteer at local events. "Our attendance each year is growing. We don't need bigger crowds. People enjoy seeing the same artists each year. And we are including a couple of new artists this year..."

The two of them were ground into their positions and not budging. Levi glanced at Erin, trying to give her the signal that it was time for the chair to step in and call halt to the whole thing. After all, their slate of artists and performers for the festival had been finalized. Nothing was going to change at this late date.

Erin nodded in response to his raised eyebrows. She held out her hands, like a traffic cop. "Thank you, Clara and Sam. I move we make a note that the issue of bringing in new artists be considered by next year's committee."

"Seconded," Levi said quickly.

A vote was taken and they finally moved on. Levi's head was pounding when Erin finally pulled the plug at eleven o'clock. "Thanks, everyone. We'll meet again on Monday and then Thursday to deal with any last-minute issues."

Two more meetings before the festival itself? Levi wanted to argue but he was too tired.

"I'm not sure I need to attend the last two meetings," he said to Erin and Oliver James, the lawyer on the committee, as they left the conference room in Erin's office. Sam and Clara had exited ahead of them, still arguing.

"My job is the same every year—it never changes," Levi

pointed out. "I organize my team to set up the booths and decorations at the beginning of the festival and then I organize my team to do the teardown at the end."

"You are officially the co-chair," Erin reminded him. "Besides, I need you to help preserve my sanity. Want to stop by my place for a nightcap?"

"Thanks, but I'm beat," Levi said.

"I'd like a drink," Oliver piped up.

Erin glanced at her phone. "Maybe Levi's got the right idea. It's later than I thought."

Levi noticed Oliver's obvious disappointment. Had Erin meant to be so dismissive? Oliver was a quiet man, small in stature, with thick dark glasses and a serious way about him. He'd moved to Woodland three years ago and Levi suspected he was having a hard time fitting in. If you hadn't grown up in them and had no children, small-town social cliques could be hard to crack.

"On the other hand, after listening to Clara and Sam argue all night, I'd say we deserve a beer." Levi clapped a hand on Oliver's shoulder. "How about O'Slattery's?"

"Yeah, sure." Oliver sounded grateful.

"I'm not going to be the only party pooper in the crowd." Erin slipped between the two men, linking arms with both of them. "O'Slattery's it is."

GRACE STEPPED INTO Dime A Cup and joined the queue at the front counter. As she waited to order her coffee and scone she scanned the crowd. Within a minute she'd spotted her. Rae Stedwell looked exactly like the photo she'd shared with Grace. Long, honey-colored hair and a fresh pretty face. She must have been watching for Grace, too, because at that same moment she stood up and waved. She was tall with a lean, athletic build, dressed in jeans and a gray Woodland High School hoodie.

Grace was surprised to see there was a guy with her. Black with crazy, curly hair and a shy smile, he looked about the same age as Rae.

When Grace joined them holding her coffee and scone, Rae stood again. "Thanks so much for meeting me, Ms. Hamilton. I'm Rae, obviously, and this is my friend Max. He kept me company on the trip up here."

The boy stood. He was even taller than Rae, all arms and legs. He gave her a nod. "I'll take off, let you two talk. But I just wanted to say that I really like your book on Central Park birds, Ms. Hamilton."

"Thank you, Max." Grace set her coffee and scone on the table so she could shake both of their hands. "You don't have to leave if you don't want to."

"This is Rae's thing," he said, emphasizing his friend's name slightly.

There was a short silence after he left.

"I like this place," Rae said, settling deeper into her chair.

Unlike most coffee shops, which seemed to favor a cozy, muted-light atmosphere, Dime A Cup was bright and spacious thanks to large south- and west-facing windows. Three open-concept levels were connected by an open-tread staircase, and Ansel Adams's prints—encased in hard plastic—were suspended at intervals from the ceiling beams.

"I'm glad," Grace said. "I'm not sure when coffee was a dime a cup...maybe in Ansel Adams's day. But the lighting...and obviously the photographs...appeal to me." She studied the high school girl more closely. Rae's gaze kept shifting from Grace, to her surroundings, to the book in front of them. Grace guessed she was a little nervous.

"I've never been interviewed for a school project before. May I say I'm honored?"

Rae smiled. "I was surprised you said yes, actually. Max didn't think you would."

"He seems like a great guy..."

A blush rose on Rae's cheeks. "He is. Um, he's not my boyfriend or anything. We've been buddies since we were little." Rae cleared her throat, then pulled a notebook from a backpack on the floor by her chair. "Anyway, I guess I should start my questions, or we'll run out of time. When did you first get interested in photography?"

Grace talked about her father, how his job as a studio photographer first got her hooked on the camera itself. "Then in high school I had this boyfriend who was really into hiking and bird watching. That probably makes him sound like a nerd, but trust me, he definitely wasn't. I'd take my camera when we went out to the local preserve, and soon I found I was hooked on taking pictures with birds."

"That's cool." Rae looked up from her notebook. "So, um, your career, it all started back in high school?"

"It sure did. I learned my photography skills from my father. But from Levi I learned how to tell stories with my pictures. When you spend enough time in nature, it changes the way you think, the way you move...and especially the way you see."

"It sounds like you really liked this guy."

"Oh, I did. But at the time I didn't realize how rare it was to have that sort of connection with someone. We...drifted apart."

Grace felt suddenly embarrassed. This girl hadn't come all this way to listen to her sad tale of lost love. Quickly she shifted the subject to all she'd learned in college, to landing her first professional gig, to getting an agent and then publishing a book. Rae asked intelligent questions and in fact, she seemed so genuinely interested that Grace had to ask, "Are you interested in photography too?"

"I'm not the artistic type. But we do have an arts festival in Woodland. Have you ever thought about coming?"

"Ah yes, the foliage arts festival." Grace gave a soft laugh. "As a young girl I dreamed about being one of the featured artists."

"Then why don't you come? It's happening next week."

"Oh, I don't know…"

"I guess it's kind of small-time for you now that you're famous?"

Grace hoped she would never be such a snob. "Most years I've just been too busy." But she wasn't this year. In fact, she'd been in an odd state of ennui since the excitement of her launch day party and then Alicia's return to Woodland.

Of course, if she went back, chances were good she'd run into Levi. He owned the local general store and was very involved in civic affairs. No doubt he'd be involved, as a sponsor or a volunteer, possibly both.

After all these years, the idea shouldn't put butterflies in her stomach.

Yet it did.

Grow up, she lectured herself. She and Levi had twenty years of different life experiences between them. What were the chances they'd still feel the same connection? Instead she should be focusing on the one person who did matter from those days. Alicia had been her stalwart supporter and friend for so long. The last surprise appearance at her book launch was just another example of her thoughtfulness and loyalty.

Whereas Grace had only met Alicia's husband Sean at their wedding and their children never.

The idea of returning to Woodland stuck with her, and thirty minutes later after Max—whom Rae was clearly crazy about despite all this talk of being friends—had returned and reminded Rae they had a train to catch, Grace texted Alicia.

Considering attending the Autumn Foliage Festival this year. Good idea?

Within seconds Alicia sent back a reply. *The one here? In Woodland???* This was followed by some astonished and excited emoji faces.

Thought it would be fun to meet your kids. But we just had a visit so...

Come! Timing is perfect. Sean just finished a small guest apartment above our garage. You can visit with us as much as you want but have some privacy.

Grace hesitated. *I suppose Levi is involved in the festival?*

Co-organizer with our mayor, Alicia fired back. *Might be good for you to see him again after all these years.*

Yes. Alicia was right. Grace had idealized her memories of Levi, set him to be so wonderful no other man could compete. Seeing him again would surely topple that myth.

You may be right, she texted back. And then, before she could chicken out, she googled the foliage festival website. Ten minutes later she'd sent an email to Clara Quiver.

"I HAVE AN exciting announcement." Clara took command of the committee meeting on Monday right after it was called to order.

Inwardly Levi groaned. He'd barely recovered from the last meeting and wasn't sure he was up for an exciting announcement of any kind.

"I've already discussed this with Erin, and she gave me the green light to sign the contract and get new stickers printed." Clara opened the cardboard box on the table in front of her and pulled out a yellow banner.

She turned it around so they could all read: "Featuring Wildlife Photographer Grace Hamilton!"

Levi stared at the name in disbelief. When Grace had first begun to have some success as a career photographer, the festival chair—at that time it was his father—had approached her to see if she would come to Woodland. The response Grace sent—via her agent—was that she regretted that she was already booked and would be out of the country.

The same thing happened the next two times Grace was invited to the festival and by the time Levi took over as chair, her name didn't even come up.

It certainly hadn't at any of their meetings for this year. So how was she suddenly the featured artist of the entire festival?

Levi glanced around the table. Both Sam and Oliver looked equally stunned by the announcement. Sam was the first to voice his concern.

"I admire Grace's work. And I'm as proud as the next guy that she hails from our small city. But didn't we agree, just one week ago, that our list of artists was finalized? We've printed posters—"

"Which is why I had these stickers made," Clara interjected. "We'll divide them up tonight and get the news out around—"

"But getting new artists was tabled for next year," Sam insisted. "So how—"

"She emailed me out of the blue." Clara's color was high, her voice pitched several tones higher than normal. "Asked if it was too late to—"

"It was too late! It is too late!" Sam said forcefully.

"I made a quick call to Erin and we agreed that an exception should be made in this circumstance." Clara turned to Erin for support.

"Grace is a local success story," Erin said. "Her latest book is a current *New York Times* bestseller. I agreed with Clara that this was too good of an opportunity to pass up. What do you think, Levi?"

If it was anyone but Grace, Levi would have said sure, no problem, he'd find a way to make the logistics of adding an extra tent work.

But it was Grace, and he found himself reluctant. If she came, there was no way he could avoid her. And he just didn't know how that would go. It might be okay. More likely it would be awkward or potentially painful.

"Well, Sam does have a point. And we've never needed a feature artist to make our festival a success." All their attending artists were local, and while many were talented, none were exactly household names.

"I'm surprised by you, Levi," Clara said using her old schoolteacher voice. "Grace used to be a good friend of yours. More than a friend, wasn't she? And you won't stick up for her now?"

"Oh?" Erin arched her eyebrows as she gave Levi a speculative look. "Were you high school sweethearts?"

"What does that matter?" Sam sounded disgusted. "The official deadline is pas—"

"I know it's past," Clara said with a note of impatience. "But think of what a draw she'll be! We've agreed she'll get a booth where she can sell signed prints of her photographs as well as copies of her new book. Isn't it amazing? We've been trying to get Grace to attend our festival for years. So unfortunate her parents moved to Florida. But at least we—"

"She just wants to promote her new book," interrupted Sam. "Where was she when—"

"And what's wrong with that?" Clara demanded. "Have you forgotten the purpose of our festival—to support artists? If you—"

Erin stood in a valiant effort to regain control. "Thank you, Clara; thank you, Sam." Then she turned to Oliver. "It looks like you're the tiebreaker. What do you think?"

Levi hadn't seen Oliver take a stand opposing any of Erin's ideas so far this year and wasn't surprised when Oliver voiced his support for including Grace Hamilton in the festival.

"That's settled then. I have to admit I wasn't expecting

this to be so contentious." Erin frowned at Levi and Sam.

Then she switched on a bright smile. "We need a picture of our committee with the new poster to share on social media." She waved at the receptionist on the other side of the glass wall and Kate Little, a friendly woman in her forties, joined them in the conference room.

Erin handed her phone to Kate. "Take lots of pictures. Make sure the sign is legible." She took one of the new banners then signaled for the rest of them to gather around.

Levi had had enough of posing for Erin's Instagram account. "I'll sit this one out."

This time Erin didn't bother frowning, she just ignored him. "Everyone get in nice and close. Kate, maybe if you stand on a chair, you'll get a better angle."

Levi knew social media was important for promoting events these days, and he gave Erin credit for being so good at it. Her skillful use of social media had probably been a big factor in getting her elected to the mayoral office.

But it wasn't for him. He still wasn't on Facebook, Instagram or Twitter, though his office manager at the store made sure Woodland General Store had an active presence. Jess told him she was glad he was a technophobe. She said her friends were constantly being embarrassed by stuff their parents posted about them.

"Thanks, Kate." Erin took back her phone and within the minute informed them she had posted the photo. "I tagged all of you—except Levi, obviously—so make sure you comment and share."

As the group dispersed, each person taking a handful of the stickers to affix to as many posters as they possibly could, Erin singled him out. "Even Sam and Clara are on Facebook. You're such a luddite." She smiled to take any sting out of the insult. "Next year I'm thinking of making social media participation a requirement of being on the committee."

"Fine with me."

She looked suspicious. "You're not going to volunteer next year, are you?"

"I'll still help with the set-up and tear-down. But sit on the organizing committee? No. That was the point of inviting you to be co-chair this year. I'd say you are more than ready to take on the full responsibility."

"So you think I'm doing a good job? Even though I let Clara add Grace Hamilton at the last minute?"

"Yes, you're doing a good job. And I may not like it myself, but you're excellent at the social media stuff."

"I realize these platforms have a negative side. But there's a lot of beauty too. It's all in what you seek. I find if you put out positivity and light, that's what you receive."

Levi believed in beauty and light, but not on the screen of his phone. He found it in the wetlands at dawn when an elegant blue heron took flight above a field of golden bulrushes. In the iridescent colors of the rufous hummingbird as it hovered over the purple blossom of a trumpet honeysuckle.

But he wasn't going to try to explain any of that to Erin.

He'd found things that mattered most to a person didn't always translate well when you put them into words.

Unless you were Grace Hamilton…

Her new book had been delivered to the store this morning and he'd spent his lunch hour gorging on it. He'd been just as impressed with the stories that accompanied each photograph as with the images themselves. She saw the joy and the tragedy in nature, the fragility and the strength, and that all of it was beautiful.

He'd followed and admired her career from a distance for years. The distance was key. It was something he wanted to preserve. She'd flown so far in her life and career, while he'd become part of the bedrock of the small town he'd never left. He doubted she ever thought of him or that he'd been any part of the equation that had made her decide to come this year.

Still, the inscription she'd chosen for the beginning of her book had given him pause. *Be true to your work, your word, and your friend*, by Henry David Thoreau. He wondered if she remembered that it was he who had introduced her to Thoreau. Not that it mattered. Henry David Thoreau was a widely quoted guy.

It was just interesting. That was all.

September 10, 1999
New York University

Dear Levi,

Loved your sketch of the yellow warbler! There's this American crow that seems determined to wake the entire dorm every morning with his ear-piercing cawing. My roommate has tried hurling things at him—shoes, books, empty beer bottles. She wants to chase him off, but I'm rooting for the crow. He reminds me of that immature raven you had eating literally out of your hand the last time we had lunch at the nature preserve. Remember what we did after that? I think about it all the time...

Chapter Four

G RACE STOOD ON Main Street, Woodland. She felt like she was in a dream or on a movie set. Instead of pinching herself she put a hand out to the brick façade of the East Central Bank. It felt solid and rough, and undeniably real, under her fingers.

She'd done it. Come home. It was a sunny day, warm for October, and the maples and oaks on the park out front of the courthouse were astonishing, in every shade of red and orange and yellow that one could imagine.

A few days from now volunteers would be erecting tents and pavilions in the park, but for now life was ordinary. Though she'd left her camera at home—deliberately because she became a different person when she had that Nikon strapped to her body—Grace found herself composing frames around the people she saw. A couple of older ladies sitting on a park bench chatting and chuckling. A father huffing, as he pushed a stroller with two children facing each other up a hill. A young woman running effortlessly with a golden retriever attached by lead to her waist.

The individual pictures added up to an idyllic scene, but

the park could only hold her interest for so long. The place she'd really come to see was across the street.

The general store was a lot as she remembered. White clapboard with a green and white striped awning over the porch. On either side of the double front doors were displays of pumpkins and autumn flowers, bins of in-season apples and pears, an American flag hung from the column to the left of the stairs. In the old days Grace knew Levi's father had replaced it with a new flag every year. It looked like Levi had continued the tradition.

Grace had walked here from Alicia and Sean's home with the expressed intention of grabbing a coffee and a piece of pie at the general store. Sean was on duty at the firehall, the boys were in school and Alicia was teaching her second yoga class of the day. Grace had attended the first and had enjoyed it a lot more than she'd expected. Regular classes of any kind were difficult to fit into her vagabond lifestyle, though.

She took a deep breath, then took the steps that led inside. The scent of the place was so familiar, instantly she felt eighteen again and instead of coffee she craved a hotdog and a Coke.

A young man stood at the till, serving a middle-aged couple. She walked down the baking supplies aisle and ended up at the lunch counter where an old friend—Connie Wilson—was taking a tray of muffins from the oven. She paused to say hello and Connie smiled.

"It's been so long! I saw your name on the posters and

could hardly believe you were coming to the festival this year."

"Too long," Grace agreed. She and Connie had drifted apart within a year of starting university. Thanks to Alicia she knew Connie had been working at the general store since her divorce about ten years ago and had recently remarried.

"I've got to get back to work, but I'll look for you at the festival," Connie promised.

"Sounds good," Grace said and continued her tour.

Toward the center of the back wall was the old black, potbelly stove, and around it were tables for two or four. One table tucked into a private nook behind the stove had a chess board painted on it and the black and white pieces were lined up, ready for a game. That was something new and it made her feel as if her heart had been squeezed.

She remembered teaching Levi the game. How smug she'd been as she beat him game after game, and then how crushed when he finally mastered the strategy enough to settle the score.

Suddenly she heard a voice over the soft country music playing on the sound system. Every nerve in her body tingled. She turned slowly in the direction of the pet food section.

And there he was. Reading the ingredient list from a can of cat food to a woman with a mop of gray hair and a canvas shopping tote. He had weathered well. His chestnut hair was still thick with that irrepressible wave that made it seem he never brushed it. He'd kept himself in shape, too. His well-muscled arms and shoulders were shown off to perfection in his short-sleeved black T-shirt with a caption she couldn't make out.

"I'll take seven cans of that one," the gray-haired lady said. She opened her tote bag and Levi dutifully added the required number. "Thank you so much, Levi. You're always so patient with me. I don't know why I never remember my reading glasses."

As she moved off, Levi must have sensed the presence of someone else, because he turned in Grace's direction. For a second he stared, quizzically. Then his eyes widened and a complicated smile—a mixture of surprise, pleasure and caution—slowly broke over his face.

"Grace."

Love, longing, loss—this man had made her feel all of these, and now, as if she were eighteen again, the cocktail of emotions flooded over her. She took a deep, long breath.

And then she noticed the quote on his T-shirt, a quip about going to a general store but not finding anything specific.

Suddenly she was laughing. "Still a fan of George Carlin."

He put a hand to his chest. "Always. The man was a genius."

"I remember laughing so hard at his monologues my stomach muscles hurt the next day."

"Best core workout ever."

As their laughter ebbed the twenty years that had passed since those days pooled in a gulf between them.

What now? Grace asked herself. Maybe she should have given this homecoming trip of hers a little more consideration.

LEVI WAS GLAD he'd been prepared to see Grace. Otherwise he might have been felled by that first glance. She'd been pretty as a teenager. But now. Now. If he was into the mayor's New Age jargon he would have said she gave off a golden aura. He'd say it anyway, because it was true.

But since he'd learned she was coming to the festival three days ago, and since Alicia had come in to buy toilet paper yesterday and managed to casually mention she was expecting a houseguest—he'd remember Grace Hamilton, of course—he'd been steeling himself for their first encounter. He hadn't expected it to be in his store. He'd imagined bumping into her on the street. Or in the park by the courthouse.

But here she was, in the pet food aisle, and he was glad because it had to mean she'd wanted to see him, or at the very worst, was not averse to seeing him. Which didn't explain why she'd suddenly gone so quiet.

"I heard you were coming to the festival this year." It

wasn't an inspired opening gambit. But he saw the relief on Grace's face and knew he'd been smart to start with something innocuous.

"Of course you did. You're on the organizing committee."

"When my dad retired from the store, he passed along more than one torch."

"Alicia told me your father retired...was it two years ago?"

"Three. He and Mom bought an RV. He said it was the only way he could let go of micromanaging the store—and me—by getting out of town. Mom was thrilled. She's always wanted to travel but with Dad's responsibilities they never got away for more than a few days at a time."

"Obviously the store is in good hands with you. I noticed the addition of the chess board table."

"You still play?"

"Not often. But if you're throwing out a challenge, then I accept."

He caught her gaze and the amused glint in her light blue eyes. "It'll have to be after hours. It doesn't do for the boss to goof around."

"Can he break for a five-minute coffee?" Grace nodded toward the lunch counter.

"Definitely." He led the way, then gestured to a couple of empty stools at the end. "Coffee? Latte?"

"I see you have an espresso machine."

Levi took pride in the gleaming stainless steel, Italian-made machine. "Took me a year to convince Dad to make the investment. What's wrong with plain coffee? he wanted to know. And he really balked when he saw the hefty price tag. But it's provided a good return on investment."

He called out to Connie, who had her back to them clearing dishes. "Hey, Connie, look who's here."

"We've already said hi," Grace said.

"Brings back lots of memories to see you two together again," Connie said.

Awkward! Levi cleared his throat. "Can you get Grace a latte please? And a slice of pie. Pumpkin, I think." He glanced back at Grace. "Still your favorite?"

"Still my favorite."

"Coming right up," Connie said.

"So." He swiveled the stool so he could look at Grace, catching a whiff of the shampoo she used. It was the same brand he remembered from high school, with a light botanical scent. "We've got a lot of catching up to do. Let's start with your book. I bought a copy last week. It's magnificent, Grace, it really is. You must be thrilled to be on the *New York Times* bestseller list."

"Thanks. I worked for five years on that book, so yes it's gratifying to have it well received. But don't think I've forgotten who first taught me that birds are more than beautiful creatures. They each have their own story to tell. I believe those were your exact words. Are you still spending lots of time at the nature reserve?"

It was gracious of her to give him even a modicum of credit. But then she'd always been that way. Her parents had done an excellent job of naming her. "My weekdays are pretty full. But on Sundays I like to hit one of the state parks for some hiking and bird watching. Chenango Valley is one of my favorites. My daughter prefers the Catskills, but that's farther so we only go there for holidays."

"Your daughter. How is she?"

"Awesome, really good. I was worried about the teenage years. So far she's a lot easier on me than I was on my parents."

Connie came over with the pie and the coffee. When Grace went for the bill, Levi covered it with his hand.

"This is on me. But I really should get back to work. Let me know when you've got time for that chess game. I've got a festival committee meeting tonight but nothing for the rest of the week."

"Yes, I know. Clara asked if I could attend."

"Really?" He'd heard nothing about that. "Well, maybe we can have a game after the meeting. It's being held here."

"I'd like that. Maybe you'll be tired enough I'll have a chance to beat you."

"You've never needed an advantage to do that."

"The last game we played was a draw. Remember?"

"I do." In fact, he was remembering too much. The first time he'd kissed her…it had been on her left knee after she'd taken a bad fall from her bike. The way his entire body would tingle when she ran her fingers through his hair—Grace had always loved to do that. And how she'd crushed his heart when she'd written that final letter from New York…

Remember that, he told himself as he was closing up his shop later that evening. *Remember that she isn't your Grace anymore, she's a star. Remember that she's leaving in a week, going back to her life*, which was so large, and leaving him here in his life, which was so small.

Not that he minded the smallness of his life. It had been his choice. His choice to move back home when Maggie got pregnant. His choice to take over the store. His choice to become the George Bailey of Woodland, a somewhat big fish in a very small pond.

As long as he remembered his place in the world—and hers—he'd be fine.

"SHE'S COMING TO Woodland, did you hear?" Max said as he handed Jess an apple. "Maybe she's even here already."

They were in her backyard, with Max up the ladder picking the ripe Cortland apples and her making sure they weren't bruised as she gently added them to the basket at her feet.

"How do you know?"

"They've revised the festival posters. Added a big yellow banner with Grace Hamilton's name."

"Oh man. Dad hasn't said a word." In hindsight she couldn't believe she'd had the nerve to go to New York City and interview her dad's ex-girlfriend under false pretense. Yes, she'd done the report on Grace's book, which sort of legitimized the trip. But she'd interviewed Grace with a fake name and hadn't been honest about why she was really there.

To check her out. And, if she passed the test—which she had with a big A plus—coerce her back to Woodland. Grace Hamilton had passed with flying colors. Now that her plan seemed to be working, Jess wasn't feeling nearly so good about herself.

"You should have talked me out of it."

"What? I tried!"

"You could have tried harder."

"But you got what you wanted. Your dad and Grace are sure to run into one another at some point in the next week. They'll fall madly in love again, and you'll be able to go to college without worrying about your dad being lonely."

Jess groaned. Her plan did sound ridiculous when he put it that way. "Don't mock me."

"Mock you about what?"

Startled by her dad's voice, Jess swung around to see him coming through the gate.

"Um…" Jess glanced at Max.

"Somehow she convinced me to pick all the apples for

her, Mr. S. Now she can't handle me teasing her about it."

"Hey, I've been helping too." Jess gave Max a grateful smile for his quick recovery, while her dad checked the quantity of apples in the basket.

"Nice job, you two. Should give us about a dozen quart jars of applesauce." He settled into a lawn chair on the cobblestone patio. "Sure is nice to come home after a long day at the store and watch someone else working for a change."

Jess threw an apple at him. "Feel free to help."

"I think I'll sit and rest for a bit longer." Her father bit into the apple.

"Was it a hard day at the store?" Jess asked tentatively.

"Not particularly."

"So…no interesting stories?"

"Mrs. Pender accidentally on purpose forgot her reading glasses again so I had to read her the ingredients on five different brands of cat food."

Jess shook her head. "Why don't you keep a pair of glasses for her at the store?"

"Because she's lonely. And pretending to forget her glasses gives her an excuse to ask for help that she doesn't really need."

Her dad was such a nice guy. Which only made Jess feel worse for deceiving him about her New York trip. And even more terrible for trying to figure out if he'd run into his ex-girlfriend yet. "So that was the highlight of the day, was it?"

"Actually..." Her dad tossed his apple core in the compost bin at the edge of the vegetable garden. "Remember that woman we were talking about last week? The one I knew in high school?"

"Uh...Grace Hamilton?"

Max jumped down from the second rung of the ladder. "The wildlife photographer?"

"So you figured that out did you?"

Jess wiped a nervous sheen of sweat from her hands to her jeans. "Her book has been in our living room forever, Dad. Though to be honest, Max made the connection, not me."

"Yeah well, Grace came by the store. So that was kind of interesting."

In the face of her father's nonchalant manner, the guilt Jess had been feeling earlier vanished. "Interesting? She was your high school sweetheart, you haven't seen her in twenty years, and that's all you have to say? It was interesting?"

"Hey, kid. Unless you want me to interrogate you about your love life—" he looked pointedly from her to Max "—you better stop asking about mine." He got up from his chair. "I'm going inside to make some burgers. Need to eat soon so I can get to my meeting. You staying for dinner, Max?"

"No thanks, Mr. S. Gotta go home. See you tomorrow, Jess."

"Really? Didn't you hear Dad say we were having burgers?" Jess hoped her teasing tone hid how much she wanted him to stay. She didn't understand why he no longer wanted to have dinner with her. Yeah, they still hung out after school a lot. But she could feel a new distance between them—and she didn't like it.

After Max left, Jess followed her father into the house and then to the kitchen where he was washing his hands at the sink. "Why did you do that?"

"What?"

"Look at Max and me as if we were...you know."

"Dating?"

She nodded.

He opened the fridge to pull out the beef patties he'd taken from the freezer that morning. "Lately I've been wondering if the two of you are heading in that direction."

Jess froze. If her dad could sense her changing feelings toward Max, did that mean Max had noticed too? Oh man, she hoped not. But if he had, it might explain why he was acting so cool. He wanted to make it clear he had no interest in being her boyfriend.

Jess almost groaned with embarrassment. "Max and I are just friends, Dad. Got it?"

Her dad gave her a look that said he saw right through her. But all he said was, "Loud and clear, kid."

September 19, 1999
New York University

Dear Levi,

I took your advice and asked my roommate if I could come to a party with her on Saturday night. We had some laughs and she introduced me to lots of people. Most of them guys, looking to hook up. When I told them I had a boyfriend, they moved on fast. I think my time is better spent with the kids in my photography classes. A couple of us from Visual Thinking went gallery hopping on Sunday afternoon. Now that was fun!

Chapter Five

"I HAD NO idea three little boys could eat so much." Grace was astonished. Not a tablespoon of the lasagna Sean had baked remained in a large casserole dish that should have served a dozen. Now Sean had taken the boys to the family room to supervise their homework, and it was up to her and Alicia to clean the kitchen.

"Can you imagine what it's going to be like when they become teens?" Alicia said. "I was thinking we could grab a glass of wine and escape to your guesthouse after dishes."

Grace looked up from wiping off the kitchen table. "Clara Quiver asked me to go to the foliage festival committee meeting tonight. Sorry, I forgot to tell you."

"Lucky you. I don't think she's mellowed a bit from her days teaching civics in high school. You better be on your best behavior." Alicia opened the dishwasher and began sliding in the dirty plates.

"There's a lot of dirty dishes. Want me to handwash some of the bigger things?"

"Everything will fit. Just watch me." Alicia winked. "This isn't my first rodeo."

Grace slotted in the cutlery. "Your family is fun. I love the way Sean teases the boys yet somehow manages to keep control over them."

"He's a pretty awesome dad. And husband. He's the whole package."

"Did you know he was the one right from the start?"

"I tried to deny it at first. I didn't want to marry a fireman. I didn't think I could handle constantly worrying about his safety. But in the end the connection between us was too strong. I just couldn't fight it."

"I'm glad you didn't. You're obviously so happy together. And you make great parents. You did good, Alicia."

"It's not too late for you to have all this." Alicia waved a hand to indicate her home, her family. She hesitated then added, "Unless you don't want it?"

Grace glanced at the doorway to the family room, wanting to make sure she couldn't be overheard. "It isn't a question of what I want anymore. Shortly after I turned thirty-five I realized the clock was ticking and so I went for a fertility test. Just to see how much time I had left. Turns out…" She took deep breath. "I didn't have any."

"Oh, Grace, honey. Why didn't you tell me this?"

"I didn't want to talk about it over the phone or in a text message. And by the next time we saw each other in person, I'd managed to convince myself it didn't matter."

Alicia hugged her. "That was a few years ago. How are you feeling about it now?"

"I've come to terms with not having children. But I am tired of being alone. I really am."

"I'm sorry. You're life looks so glamorous to me. I didn't realize you were unhappy."

Until she'd finished this last book, Grace hadn't realized it herself. "Traveling is lonely, but sometimes Manhattan is even worse. I mean, my closest friend is a seventy-year-old retired stage manager for Pete's sake!"

"Harvey's great, but I agree he's not dating material. What about that photographer you were seeing last year? Andrew Warner?"

"That was off and on—I was away so much shooting for my national parks book. We just sort of drifted apart."

"Like you always do."

"Something always feels like it's missing."

Grace didn't need to say anything more. Alicia knew what her problem was.

"You haven't had a chance to tell me how things went at the general store," Alicia said. "Did you get a chance to talk to Levi?"

"Briefly."

Alicia put a hand on her hip. "And…?"

"He still seems pretty awesome. At least to me." So much for hoping she would take one look at him and wonder why she had ever thought he was special.

"Levi is a great guy," Alicia agreed. "Maybe this is your second chance with him?"

"I'm surprised he didn't remarry. His wife's been gone a long time."

"Believe me there are several women in town who have tried to tempt him back to the altar. The current odds on favorite is our mayor—Erin Powers."

"Oh? She's on the festival committee too, isn't she?"

Alicia nodded. "She's kind of a dynamo around town. I know her quite well because she comes to my afternoon power yoga class. Besides being mayor she's also Woodland's top Realtor. She's beautiful and in great shape, and she makes the most of it on her very active Instagram account where she promotes using positive thinking to manifest your destiny."

"So how has Levi managed to resist this paragon?"

"Maybe he's waiting for Jess to leave for college. Or…" Alicia winked "…maybe he's been waiting for you. Did he mention anything about seeing you again? Outside of the festival, I mean?"

"He did mention playing chess together."

Alicia rolled her eyes. "You guys always did the most boring stuff together. Maybe he is the one for you. And if not, then you've got to learn to let him go."

AFTER A QUICK dinner with his daughter, Levi hurried back to the store to put on a pot of coffee and slice some of the day's leftover pastries.

Clara Quiver and Sam Rigby arrived within five minutes of each other and immediately set to arguing about the size of the booth Clara had planned for Grace Hamilton.

"It's not fair to the other artists who attend every year if we treat Grace Hamilton like some sort of queen," Sam said. "I don't see why—"

"We agreed we would bring her in as a special guest. That should come with perks. And let's face it, she's going to be a bigger draw than the others. She needs more—"

"Let's ask Levi for his opinion," Sam countered.

"Consider me Switzerland." Levi did not understand why two intelligent people with similar interests—they were both former educators and also very active in the local duplicate bridge chapter—had to be at odds so much.

"I've redone the schematic." Clara pulled a large roll of paper from a cardboard tube and then laid it flat on the luncheon counter. When Sam grunted his disapproval, she turned to Levi. "What do you think?"

Levi studied the plan and quickly located Grace's booth. As Sam had complained, it was indeed the largest and was situated on prime real estate, near the gazebo where various musical acts would be performing at intervals throughout the festival.

Before he could make any comment, Erin walked in with Oliver James, followed thirty seconds later, by Grace. The mayor looked polished and well-groomed in an eye-popping turquoise dress, with lots of matching jewelry. But to Levi, the elegant woman a few steps behind her, in dark blue jeans, a cream-colored cashmere sweater and a single gold chain, was far more captivating.

"Hi, Grace."

"Levi."

There was something almost shy about her smile, which he found adorable. When they were teenagers Grace had always found meeting new people and social events intimidating. Even in college she hadn't been keen on the socializing side of things.

He was about to offer Grace a coffee when Erin stepped between them.

"Hi, Grace, I'm Erin Powers the committee chair. It's so wonderful to meet you. Unlike some on our committee—" she glanced pointedly at Levi "—I was thrilled when Clara said you were interested in taking part in our festival."

"Some weren't thrilled then?" Grace gave Levi a look that requested an explanation.

"Now that you're here, everyone is thrilled," Levi assured her, hoping Sam wouldn't jump in and contradict him. But it seemed Sam had been charmed.

"We are indeed."

"I hear you and Levi were once an item," Erin said. "Before he married Maggie."

"My interest in ornithology is all thanks to Levi," Grace said. "We spent a lot of time...hiking in the nature preserves and state parks around here."

Erin's confident smile wavered at the deliberate pause in Grace's sentence, the intimation that she and Levi had done a lot more than just hike, which of course they had. With businesslike crispness she introduced the other committee members and explained their roles to Grace.

"We've never had a big-name artist at our festival before," Erin continued. "We're hoping this year's event will draw record-breaking crowds."

Levi took that moment to invite everyone to help themselves to coffee. "It's decaf. And there are some pastries too."

Everyone took him up on his offer before settling in. Levi had pushed several tables together to make space for six people. Erin took her place at the head and gestured for Grace to sit on her left. When Levi tried to take the seat opposite Grace, Erin objected.

"You're co-chair so you should sit at the other head," Erin said, gesturing to the far end of the table. Rather than point out that there could not be two heads of a table, Levi simply complied, while Oliver, Clara and Sam occupied the middle seats.

"First I want to welcome Grace officially to the Woodland Autumn Foliage Festival," Erin began. "We're excited to have an *New York Times* bestselling author and world-class photographer at our event." Erin paused to smile at Grace, but there was a hint of caution behind the smile.

It seemed Erin was losing some of her enthusiasm for her

special guest.

Erin went through the itinerary for the event. "I'll do a short introduction of Grace at the cocktail reception on Friday night." Erin turned to face Grace. "Then you can mingle with the other artists and of course, our sponsors."

Levi wondered if anyone else noticed the faint frown line form on Grace's forehead.

"Cocktail reception? Clara didn't mention anything about that."

"It's not usual for the artists to attend," Clara said. "But you're special and there are perks to being the guest of honor."

To Levi it seemed obvious that Grace would rather not have those perks. But she simply nodded her acceptance of the plan.

Erin cleared her throat, regaining control of the meeting. "On Saturday you'll be in your booth for the majority of the day, though you should feel free to take breaks when you need them. Then at the banquet on Saturday night you'll have an opportunity to say a few words."

Grace's eyebrows went up. Clearly this hadn't been discussed either. She glanced from Erin to Clara, then let out a long breath before saying quietly, "I'd be honored."

Once Erin finished with the itinerary, Sam raised the issue of the booth sizes. As he and Clara began arguing again, Levi got up to refill his coffee cup. A moment later Grace joined him.

"Scrappy group you've got here."

He poured coffee for her. "Those two live to argue with one another. Are you sure you're okay with the cocktail party and the little speech on Saturday? I can get you out of both if you want."

"That's okay. Mixing and mingling and public speaking are not my favorite things, as you know. But in my career I've had to learn to put up with them now and then."

Levi noticed Erin frowning at them. He put a hand to Grace's elbow and guided her back to their chairs.

An hour later when the meeting was over, Erin asked if anyone was interested in heading to the pub for a nightcap.

"It's late for me," Clara said.

"I agree with Clara," Sam said. "Want me to walk you home?"

"That would be nice. Thanks, Sam."

Grace raised her brows. "That seemed awfully pleasant."

"They're good friends when they don't have anything to fight about," Levi said.

"About that drink," Oliver said. "I'm game. Grace?"

"I'm going to help Levi clean up here," Grace said.

"Maybe we should all stay and help," Erin said, but Levi shook his head.

"There's not much to do. Why don't you and Oliver go on without us?"

Erin didn't look happy, but she took the hint and the two of them left.

"I feel weird," Grace confessed as she handed him coffee cups to load into the dishwasher. "Everyone making such a fuss over me."

"You're a big deal. You get that don't you?"

"When you're boot-deep in mud, waiting for the sun to rise so you can get that perfect shot of a white trumpeter swan against a tangerine sky, you don't feel like a big deal."

"I guess that's the definition of being grounded."

She chuckled. "You and your puns."

Levi started the dishwasher, then turned to study Grace. Back in high school some of his friends had considered her cool and reserved. They thought because she was beautiful and talented that she thought she was better than the rest of them.

But it was actually the opposite that was true. She'd simply been shy, an introvert, with a strong streak of humility. He was intrigued that all her success didn't seem to have changed those fundamental elements of her character.

"The meeting went late, as usual. Are you still up for a game?"

Without bothering to answer, Grace went to the chess table and fisted a black and a white pawn. She put her hands behind her body for a few moments, then held out her hands for him to choose.

He chose black.

Time seemed to fall away as they set up the board and then began to play. Grace had always been a fan of the rook opening, but she surprised him by offering the queen's gambit, which he refused. From that moment on, all his concentration was on the board. After about an hour he blundered and lost his first rook.

That was the beginning of the end as Grace expertly tightened the noose. With reluctance he laid down his queen. "I see where this is headed. Well done, Grace."

"Thank you. This is a lovely chess set. Do you remember the awful one we used to play on? The board was flimsy cardboard and the pieces were plastic."

"But it was portable—that was the thing." He'd kept it in his backpack and they'd played outside when the weather was good, in the library or back seat of his Jeep when it wasn't.

They'd done other things outside and in the back seat of his Jeep, too.

He gazed into her eyes, still such a pure blue it didn't seem possible they were natural. "Seeing you again is bringing back a lot of memories."

"For me too."

Her smile was warm and seemed to suggest that the memories were good. And most of them were. As Levi walked her to her car, he was overwhelmed with the desire to pull her into his arms and kiss her. But he was a thirty-eight-year-old man, with a teenaged daughter, aging parents, and a small-town general store. What did he have to offer a woman like Grace?

But after they'd said goodbye and he'd watched her drive off, he couldn't help but grin, and the silly, happy smile was still on his face when he went to bed twenty minutes later.

THE NEXT MORNING Levi woke earlier than usual so he could rake leaves at his parents' place before opening the store. His parents lived on a huge lot with several massive oak trees, almost a quarter acre of lawn to mow, and a large driveway to shovel in the winter. Levi didn't mind the extra work—he loved his folks and they had done a lot for him. He just worried if he didn't do the garden chores fast enough, his father would step in when he shouldn't.

As he gathered up the mounds of leaves, Levi's mind drifted to Grace and the way she'd sought him out at the meeting last night. Going for a coffee refill at the same time he did, then staying late to help clean up and play that game of chess. He supposed it was only natural that she'd feel comfortable around him, even after all these years. He shouldn't read anything but friendship into her actions.

When he was finished bagging the leaves, he went into the house where his parents were having coffee in the sunroom that adjoined the kitchen.

"I was going to take care of those leaves this afternoon," his father said, not looking up from his crossword. "I'm perfectly capable of raking you know."

Levi didn't argue, even though the specialist had been quite clear about walking being the most vigorous exercise his father should undertake. He helped himself to a coffee and a piece of toast from a pile at the center of the table.

"Well, I think it was very thoughtful of you, Levi," his mother said, frowning at his dad. "Those trees sure put out a prodigious amount of leaves."

His father grunted. "Three letter word for 'bowler.'"

"Nut," his mother supplied. When both men turned to her, confused, she shrugged. "I think anyone who likes bowling is nuts."

"Hat," his father said. Then jotted down the answer.

Love of puns must run in the family, Levi reflected, remembering Grace's comment from the other day.

"So what are you guys up to today?" he asked.

"Why ask me?" his dad grumbled. "I'm too sick to do anything."

"Oh, Pat. I'm baking apple pies with those lovely Cortlands Jess brought over last night."

Only then did Levi notice the basket of apples on the counter. "She must have done that while I was at the festival meeting."

"She's such a sweet girl. I'm really going to miss her when she starts college."

"That's one thing we can all agree on," his father said. A timer went off on his cell phone and he sighed. "Time for my pills. Excuse me a minute."

"I guess it's part of the parenting gig, huh?" Levi reflected, as his father left the room. "Letting them go when the time comes."

"Your father and I were lucky. You came back after college. I have to admit I worried that you might get distracted."

"This wouldn't be about Grace Hamilton would it?" His mom hadn't liked Grace much when they were kids. At the time he hadn't understood why, but he'd grown to understand that, even back then, Grace's talent and ambition had been obvious. Her aspiration to be a photographer and to travel the world was not what his parents—especially his mother—wanted for him.

"Well, I did hear she's back in town for the festival. I remember how inseparable the two of you once were."

"That was a long time ago."

"It was. I just hope she doesn't turn your head again. Not when there are so many lovely local women available."

Levi shook his head. "Don't go there, Mom."

His mother wisely changed the subject. "Jess talked about Max quite a bit last night. Do you think after all these years they've become romantically interested in each other?"

"I suspect Jess is ready for that. I'm not sure her feelings are reciprocated. Max has been different lately. He used to eat half his evening meals at our house. But not lately."

"You think maybe he's involved with a different girl?"

"If so, he hasn't told Jess. I hope it's not the case. I'd really hate to see her hurt."

His mother raised her eyebrows. "So now you know how I feel."

"About Jess and Max?"

"No. You and Grace. Be careful, Levi. That's all I'm asking."

September 22, 1999
New York University

Dear Levi,

So. Big news. My dad got a new job in Tampa and the family is moving back to Florida. I thought it would happen one day. Mom hasn't stopped complaining about New England winters since we moved to Woodland when I was in seventh grade. I'll never forget how lonely I felt that first week. Everything changed when you picked me to be your science partner. Do you remember how we were the only ones who managed to get our battery to work on the first try? We were an awesome duo right from the start!

Chapter Six

THE MORNING AFTER the committee meeting, Grace slipped out of the guesthouse with her camera slung over her torso. She'd learned it was better for all concerned to avoid Alicia and Sean's house when they were getting the boys ready for school.

She strolled from the Morettis' house down to the walking path that followed Woodland Creek as it meandered through town. If she followed it to the right, she would eventually reach the falls and the campground and swimming hole she'd enjoyed so much as a teen. Maybe tomorrow she would take that route. But today she turned left.

Last night she'd had trouble sleeping. She hadn't expected things to feel so good and natural with Levi. He got all her jokes. He knew all her foibles. His merest touch still gave her shivers. Suddenly she wasn't so sure her reasons for wanting to see him again were very sound.

What if she ended up falling in love with him again?

Would it end any different a second time? She couldn't imagine him coming to New York with her. And she sure didn't belong here in Woodland.

Grace tried to clear her mind and enjoy her surroundings. During the six years her family had lived in Woodland, she'd never really felt like she belonged. Most of the kids at school had known each other since kindergarten. Though she'd eventually made friends...Levi, Alicia and Connie...Woodland itself had been a place to escape from. She'd longed for the excitement of New York City and the prospect of exotic travels as a photojournalist.

As a teenager she hadn't appreciated the simple pleasures Woodland had to offer. Now she couldn't take ten steps without seeing something she wanted to photograph. A red-leaved sugar maple reflected perfectly along a quiet edge of the creek. A shy dark-eyed junco foraging among the undergrowth. An old-fashioned red mailbox at the end of someone's lane. Eventually she left the path and wound her way through the neighborhood where she'd grown up.

She'd just reached her family's former house when she noticed a tall, lanky man carrying a rake and walking in her direction. She liked the way he moved, his naturally athletic gait, the extra bit of spring in his steps. At some point she realized it was Levi.

She could tell the moment he spotted her back. First he paused. Then smiled and hurried forward.

"You're out early," he said.

"Wanted to catch the morning light. I'd forgotten how pretty this town is." She eyed the rake. "Trying to earn some extra cash?"

He chuckled. "I was just at my folks', cleaning up their yard before I open the store. So what do you think of the old house?" He nodded at the structure in front of them. "It's been painted a few times. New roof too, I believe. But other than that, it hasn't changed much."

"No, it hasn't. I have this odd feeling that if I went through the front door I'd be transported back to when I was eighteen and find everything exactly the way it was then."

"Want to test your theory?" Levi nodded at the entrance.

She laughed. "I'd probably be arrested."

"Guess we better move along then, before the owners notice us gawking. I'm on my way to work. You?"

"I'm heading to Main Street too. I'd like to take some photos. Maybe get a latte from a place I know." She bumped her shoulder against his and instead of bumping her back, the way he used to do when they were younger, he gave her this long, intense look. His gaze pierced through the thick protective layers that separated them, making Grace remember how it had been for them when they were younger, and every touch had been charged with so much sexual energy.

That energy was back, and she was certain he was going to kiss her.

But all he did was suggest they walk together. "As long as you don't mind being seen with a rake."

It took her a moment to spot the pun. This time she groaned. "Really, Levi?"

"I can't help it. It's genetic. Take it up with my dad."

"So…the meeting last night. That was pretty intense."

"The Autumn Foliage Festival is serious business in this town. It's the highlight of our peak tourist season."

"I remember going as a kid. I just never appreciated how much work was involved."

"Things will really get crazy on Thursday," Levi said. "That's when my sub-committee will start setting up the booths, signage and decorations. Port-a-potties and garbage bins come Friday morning."

"You're going to be so busy. I was hoping you'd let me beat you again at chess. Also I'd love to get out for a hike while I'm in town. But it doesn't sound like you'll have time."

"I can make time. How about Wednesday?"

"Tomorrow? But don't you have to work?"

"My staff can manage the store for a day without me."

"I'm glad."

"Me too. Fall migration is such an interesting time for bird watching. You never know what you'll find."

She gave him a second look. Was it just the fall migration that made him so willing to change his schedule for her? Judging by the sparks a minute ago, she didn't think so.

"SO HOW FAR are we running today?" Jess caught up with Max outside the west door after school ended for the day. He looked cool in ripped jeans and a tight long-sleeved T-shirt that showed off his strong, lean physique.

She felt a secret thrill that he'd been waiting for her. She knew many of her girlfriends were jealous. "He's so devoted," they said. When she protested they were just friends, the answer she got back was, "Yeah, right."

"Max?" He'd started walking as soon as she caught up to him, head bowed, mind clearly somewhere else. "Our run?"

"Oh, um, I forgot about that. Let me check." He pulled his phone out of his back pocket. "Supposed to be eight miles today. But we could make it up later in the week."

"Skip a run?" He'd never suggested such a thing before. "What's going on with you?"

"Nothing. I just thought it wouldn't hurt if we missed a run. That's all."

"Do you still want to do the Spring Fling marathon together in April?"

"Yeah, of course I do."

Where was his normal enthusiasm? "Cause the marathon was your idea. And you're the one who drew up our training schedule. And told me I had to take it seriously and not skip a run just because I wasn't in the mood."

"Yeah, yeah, I know. You're right. I'm just not up to running today."

"Fine," she said, but she didn't feel fine. She knew things were going to change between her and Max once they started college. But she hadn't expected things to start changing already.

It wasn't just his unusual disinterest today. Or the way he never stayed for dinner anymore. He was also texting her a lot less frequently in the evenings. Max was drifting away from her at the exact time that she wanted him to be closer. She was scared to ask him what the problem was. What if she ended up pushing him even further away?

"So what do you want to do?" Max asked as they neared her house. "Want to play Fortnite? Binge-watch cat videos?"

"I just got a text from Dad. He wants me to put some potatoes in the oven to bake. After that we can play Fortnite if you want." Max followed as Jess marched up the porch steps, unlocked the front door and headed to the kitchen. While she scrubbed the potatoes and pricked them with a fork, Max tore off two pieces of aluminum foil.

"Want me to put in a potato for you? We're having these with Dad's baked beans and coleslaw." Both of which were favorites of Max.

"Can't. Thanks though."

She stared at him. "I thought Dad's baked beans were your absolute favorite."

"They are. I've just got other places to be, okay?"

She strove to hide her hurt feelings and keep her tone casual. "I can't remember the last time you stayed for dinner. You used to be here three or four nights a week. What's up?"

Max drummed his fingers on the countertop. "Just hanging close to home."

Jess waited, but he didn't say anything else.

WEDNESDAY MORNING LEVI woke up with an unaccustomed giddy feeling in the pit of his stomach. He felt like a kid about to play hooky from school.

Jess was unusually quiet at the breakfast table. Come to think of it, she'd been quiet last night, too.

"Everything okay?"

She stirred her yogurt with no apparent interest in eating it. "Max is being so weird lately. Have you noticed?"

Levi hesitated. "Have you tried talking to him about it?"

"He says he's just spending more time at home. But—"

"Are you worried he's out with other friends? Maybe…a girl?"

She nodded. "It would be okay if he was."

Levi doubted that.

"I just wish he was being honest with me."

"Maybe it's time you made an effort to go out with your other friends more often?" Jess and Max both hung out with a group of mutual friends on Friday and Saturday nights, but they normally just saw each other the rest of the time.

"I could do that," she agreed.

But she didn't look excited about it. Levi wished his daughter would tell him how she really felt about Max. Then he might be able to offer her some better guidance. Or could he? He was pretty rusty at this dating business. So rusty he wasn't even sure if his plans with Grace today could be considered a date.

Whoa. Where had that thought come from? Their hike today was definitely not a date. He went back to studying his daughter, who looked no happier after his well-intentioned attempt to talk to her.

"Want me to drop you off at school today?"

"You're driving to work?"

He almost always walked when the weather was decent. "No. I'm taking the day off. Going to the Westland Nature Preserve." He forced himself to add—because if he wanted honesty from Jess, he ought to offer it himself: "With Grace."

"Oh. That was fast work, Dad."

"She suggested it. She's hoping to get some shots of some rare birds."

"Uh-huh." Jess's tone was teasing. "Just make safe choices, Dad."

"I KNOW IT'S cliché but I just have to say it. This feels like old times." Grace was in the passenger seat of his Ford F-150, windows open and music from the New Radicals playing on the sound system.

"Yup. On the highway, headed for adventure." With a

pretty woman by my side, he thought but didn't say.

"This new truck is pretty swank. What happened to your old Jeep?"

"Pretty much fell apart the year Maggie and I got married. But I got a lot of good years out of it."

"Yes." She was silent for a moment. When she spoke next her tone was subdued. "About your wife. Maggie. We haven't spoken since she died, and I've never had a chance to tell you how sad I was for you and your daughter. I can't imagine how hard that was."

For a long time Levi had been unable to speak about Maggie's death without experiencing visceral, gut-wrenching pain. But his grief had dulled over time, just as his parents had told him it would. "I felt pretty angry for a time. All it took was a patch of black ice and a deer on the road and she was gone. It seemed more than unfair. I felt like it was something God—or fate—had done deliberately to hurt me. And what made it even more unbearable was knowing my daughter would have to grow up without a mother."

"It was unfair," Grace agreed. "So unfair."

"I got past the resentment. I had to. It wasn't possible to be angry and bitter and be a good father to Jess too. So, while it was challenging being a single parent, having a kid to worry about also kind of saved me."

"Jessica is lucky to have a dad like you, Levi."

"I couldn't have done it without my folks. They helped so much, especially when Jess was too young for school."

"Even so. Being a single parent seems pretty daunting to me."

"Is it something you've ever considered?" Levi asked. "Being a parent...single or otherwise?"

"Not in the cards for me, I'm afraid."

Her tone seemed artificially light. He waited to see if she would say more on the subject. She didn't.

"What about marriage?"

"Relationships are challenging when you travel as much as I do. What about you? You've been a widower a long time."

"Between the store and Jess and looking after my folks I don't have much spare time. I had a buddy get divorced and then remarried. He had kids with the new wife and that was great. But it seemed to me that the kids from his first marriage got shortchanged."

"And you didn't want that to happen to your daughter?"

"Exactly. She'd lost her mother. I never wanted her to feel like she'd lost her father too."

"You must have been lonely though. At times?"

He shrugged. "I'm not complaining. I really got to enjoy all it means to be a father, to raise a child." He shot her an uncomfortable look. "Sorry, I hope you don't take that as some sort of judgment on you. Not having kids, I mean."

"That's okay. It wasn't a decision I necessarily made. It's just the way life has turned out for me."

Levi had a sense there was more to this story. But they

had reached their destination and he let the subject drop.

There were no other vehicles in the small parking lot. Coming very early in the middle of the week was working in their favor. They got out of the truck, grabbed their gear.

"I feel so happy to be here," Grace said.

"Me, too." He loved the way he felt at the beginning of a hike, the anticipatory buzz. What would they see today? Anything was possible.

Making it all so much better was having Grace by his side. It felt so natural and right, as if only weeks, not years, had passed since they last went trekking together.

They slipped on their backpacks. Grace slung her camera around her neck, and he did the same with his field binoculars.

"Want to do the full circuit?" Grace asked him.

He didn't answer for a moment. He was struck how, even in basic hiking clothing, there was something so elegant about her. Being tall and lean helped. But it was also the way she moved, her poise and adroitness.

She asked again, "The circuit?"

He refocused. There was a network of trails through the preserve, but the circuit touched on all the main habitats...the woodlands, the pond, the marsh and the meadow.

"That would be perfect."

Whenever he was out looking for birds, Levi liked to imagine he was a mountain lion, moving silently and stealthily along the path. In his experience most hikers were careless and loud. They created a wake not unlike that of a motor-boat—pushing out the birds and other animals who would hide until the disturbance had passed.

Grace, like him, had perfected this way of movement through the forest and he could barely hear her footsteps as they traveled abreast on the dirt path. The multi-colored leaves of the deciduous forest at this time of year were beautiful but they also provided excellent camouflage to the foraging birds.

Levi tuned in to the sounds of the forest. The distinctive song of the eastern wood peewee led them to a juvenile, perched on a branch of a red oak, on the lookout for insects. Next he and Grace traced the distinctive drumming of a woodpecker to a female yellow-bellied sapsucker. When they reached the border of the marsh Grace froze and touched his arm—their long-ago signal that something interesting had been spotted.

Levi followed her gaze to a low point in the thicket. A flash of yellow caught his eye. Sure enough a male common yellowthroat was feeding on the lower branches of a black willow. Levi slowly brought his binoculars to his eyes while Grace did the same with her camera.

The shy yellowthroat was small with a rounded belly. His striking black mask contrasted beautifully with his bright yellow throat. Levi hoped Grace was getting some good pictures.

By lunchtime they reached the meadow. It felt natural to

gravitate to the same grouping of rocks where they had stopped for picnics when they were young.

Levi pulled out pita pockets packed with falafel, chopped veggies and tahini sauce. Grace had a thermos of iced tea to share. They sat side by side, munched their food quietly, watching as a half-dozen robins, about fifty feet away, pecked at the grass in their hunt for worms.

When they were finished eating, Grace stretched out on the ground, using her backpack as a pillow.

"Is your daughter going to college next year?"

"That's the plan and I hope she does. If she had her way, though, she'd stay in Woodland and work full-time at the store."

"Do you think she's trying to please you?"

"I hope not. The business will be hers one day if she wants it. But only if she wants it. I've always been very clear on that with her."

"Unlike your own parents," Grace said softly.

Levi couldn't deny it—Grace had been around his family enough to know how it had been—but he felt bound to defend his parents. "Not every kid is lucky enough to get handed a family business. And it's worked out well. I've had a great life."

"You're talking as if you're seventy, Levi."

"I'm not?"

She smiled and shook her head. "You're impossible." She hesitated then added, "Ever wonder what our lives would be like if we hadn't broken up?"

"We went our separate ways for good reasons. My path led to my daughter and to a rewarding life in a town I love. Yours has taken you to an amazing career and experiences I can only imagine."

"True." Grace sounded resigned, if not disappointed by his answer.

Levi touched the side of her head, brushed back the hair that gleamed like gold in the noon sun. "It's kind of shocking how good it feels to be with you here. I guess I thought the twenty years we've spent apart would have created more of a barrier. But—you're still you."

She turned so she could see his face. "And you are still you."

He sensed she wanted him to kiss her, and Lord did he want to. But something made him hold back. Was it the things his mother had said yesterday? Or Jess reminding him to make safe choices?

No, much as he loved them both, it was his own voice of caution that was sounding out the warning.

"You're so beautiful Grace. I can't believe you have any time for a small-town guy like me."

"What's so wrong with a small-town guy? When I was young, I didn't think you'd be hard to replace. I thought I'd fall in love a bunch of times in my life before I settled down. But I was wrong. What we had was more rare than I appreciated."

"I feel the same."

"You married. Had a child. Obviously I wasn't that hard to forget."

She seemed to forget that she hadn't given him much choice but to forget her. "Maggie was sweet. I was lucky to find her. I'm sorry you haven't been as fortunate."

"I've met a lot of interesting men. But life always seems to pull us in opposite directions. It's probably my career. I don't just love it. I've been consumed by it. I guess that makes me pretty selfish."

"No. It makes you complicated. And fascinating."

As their gazes connected again, Levi found himself drawn to her in a way he hadn't felt for a very long time. She sat up and he brushed some crushed leaves and bits of grass from her back. He wanted to keep touching her. To tangle his hands in her hair and pull her mouth to his.

He was inches from kissing her when he sensed movement in the tall grasses to his right.

Grace had spotted it too. "Oh wow, Levi. I think that's a Henslow's sparrow. I haven't seen one of those in years."

For once Levi was not excited by a rare bird sighting. Slowly he reached for his binoculars and trained them on the small, dull-colored bird. His first thought was grasshopper sparrow. But as he focused on the delicate black markings on the olive-colored face, he saw that was wrong. "Sure looks like it."

Grace was already crouched in the grass, taking pictures.

He watched her work, as absorbed in her as she was in the sparrow.

Sometimes, he reflected, what brought you together could also tear you apart. It was probably for the best he hadn't kissed her.

Later, on the drive home, Grace got a call. When she glanced at the screen she apologized. "Sorry, I have to take this."

He nodded, kept his eyes on the road.

"Jeremy. Good to hear from you."

A man's voice rumbled on the other end of the line. Levi tried to distract himself with other thoughts. He noted a flock of Canadian geese in classic V-formation flying to his left. Then speculated on how things had gone at the store in his absence.

At least five minutes passed before Grace spoke again. "That sounds fabulous. Look, I'm with someone right now. Can I call you back tomorrow?"

Levi tightened his grip on the steering wheel. Whatever that call had been about was none of his business and he wasn't going to ask any questions. But Grace wasn't reticent.

"That was Jeremy Browne, my agent. There's an opportunity for me to work on a project in Costa Rica the first three weeks of November."

"Sounds exciting."

Her face glowed. "You would love Costa Rica. As soon as you step off the plane you can feel and smell the difference in the air. The vegetation is so lush and wild. And the birds! You've never seen such colors or fascinating personalities."

He may not have visited in person, but he'd devoured many articles featuring tropical birds of Central and South America, so he had an idea of what was out there. "I'll go one day."

"What about now?" Grace twisted in her seat so she could face him. Eyes bright, she put a hand on his shoulder. "Come with me. I'm serious. I could probably get your travel costs covered if you were willing to help with the project."

The idea electrified him, but only for a moment. Grace was obviously used to flitting from one location to another—all she needed was a passport and her damn camera.

"I can't," he said, his voice flat.

"But you haven't even considered the idea. Couldn't Jessica stay with her grandparents? And you said you had an assistant at the store."

She didn't get it.

"You're asking me to vacate my life for three weeks when I've never left Jessica for a day, let alone three weeks. And the most I've stepped away from the store is four days. Then there's my parents. They're getting older. They need me now, too."

Silence stretched as Grace simply sat there, absorbing his words and studying his face. When she spoke again, her tone was subdued.

"If the idea doesn't appeal to you, just say so. You don't

need to list a bunch of excuses."

Levi hated that he'd made his responsibilities in life sound like chains, when in fact, Jessica, the store and his parents were the very things that gave his life meaning.

"I wasn't giving excuses. I was describing my life. It may seem pedestrian to you. But not to me."

Grace shifted in her seat so she was facing the road again. "I'm sorry. I didn't mean to imply your life wasn't important. I just thought you might like to see Costa Rica."

He did. Which, for some reason, only made Levi feel more angry.

September 30, 1999
New York University

Dear Levi,

No, of course I don't want to go to Florida for Thanksgiving. I want to go to Woodland and see you. Connie said I can stay at her house—I just hope she doesn't interfere too much with our plans. I already told her I've been invited to your place for Thanksgiving dinner. Which was nice of your mom. You shouldn't be surprised she didn't like the idea of me staying for the entire weekend. She's never been my biggest fan. She's afraid I'll lure you to the Big Apple and corrupt you!

Chapter Seven

J ESS WAS AT her father's desk in the back room of the store
when she heard a tap on the door and her grandmother's
voice.

"You in there, honey?"

"Sure am, Grams."

The door opened and her grandmother came in dressed
in the jogging pants and zip-up hoodie she wore when she
went walking with her friends.

"The girls—" her grandmother still called her friends
"girls" even though they were all women in their sixties "—
and I just came in for a coffee after our walk and Connie
mentioned you were working today."

"Yup. Matching up the shipping receipts and the invoic-
es before we pay the bills." At least she was trying. She was
having a hard time focusing. That seemed to be the case no
matter what she was doing these days.

Jess had worked in the family store for as long as she
could remember. She'd done all the jobs: dusting shelves and
sweeping the front porch when she was little, then stocking
inventory and working the till. The past few years she'd been

learning the accounting program her father used and had even prepared the draft financials and income tax return last year.

While she was prepared to admit that taking business admin in college would make her even better equipped to run the store one day, she also felt that she could get by without it.

Her grandmother sat in the empty chair on the other side of the desk. "I hear your father took today off work. That's not like him."

"No. He should do it more often." Several times a year the two of them went away on long weekends. When she was little they'd gone to Disney World a few times, also to a cabin on Lake George. But the maximum time they'd spent away from Woodland—and the store—was four nights.

"I agree. Your father works far too hard." Her grandmother pinched her right earlobe, a sign she was worried. "Do you know where he's gone today?"

"He took Grace out to the Westland Preserve. They'll probably go to the meadow, have a picnic lunch and then complete the circuit." Jess checked the time on her phone. "He should be back any minute."

But her grandmother wasn't interested in when he would be back. "Grace Hamilton," she sighed. "She's hardly back in Woodland and already your father has taken up with her again."

Jess had expected her grandmother to be pleased. "I

thought you wanted Dad to start dating again?"

"I do. With some nice, local woman. Our mayor, for instance, would be perfect. I follow Erin on Instagram and she's always so positive and upbeat. I was so happy when he invited her to co-chair the committee with him this year. I thought it was a sign he was interested in her."

"I don't know, Grams. Dad told me he wanted to mentor the mayor so she could take over the committee next year."

"Nothing more than that?"

"Don't think so. At dinner the other night he said she wasn't his type."

"Oh dear. And now he's out with Grace. This is not good."

"What do you have against Grace? From what I've se—" Jess caught herself just in time "—heard. From what I've heard they share a lot of similar interests."

"I suppose. But your father very sensibly kept his interest in birding and sketching as a hobby, unlike Grace who is a real wanderer."

Gram's gaze went to the bulletin board on the wall behind Jess where her father pinned some of his favorite ink drawings of birds. There was also a drawing of Jess as a baby and she liked to tease her father that he had always thought of her as his little chick.

"But aren't you impressed with how successful Grace has been?" she pressed her grandmother.

Grams compressed her lips and shook her head. "She may have published some books and made a name for herself in the photography world but look at the price she paid. No family. No children. I bet she's away traveling more days than she spends at home. How could that lifestyle possibly mesh with your father's?"

"No offense, Grams, but that's a really old-fashioned way of thinking. A woman is allowed to choose a career over babies."

"Maybe it is old-fashioned. Family. Community. These things don't matter to people anymore. But they matter to your grandfather and me, and I hope they still matter to your father. Because it would break my heart if he decided, after all these years, that he was going to follow Grace back to New York City."

Guilt welled up in Jess's chest. If that happened, it would be on her. Jess hoped her grandmother never found out it was her fault Grace Hamilton had come back to Woodland. "If they did get back together, maybe it will end differently. Maybe Grace would move here?"

Grams raised her eyebrows skeptically. "I don't see that happening. But I've already said my piece to your father so now I'd best butt out." Slowly her grandmother got to her feet, but she paused on her way to the door.

"Where's your friend Max? I thought the two of you always hung out together after school?"

"He had something to do. He didn't say what."

"You sound unhappy."

Jess swiveled back and forth in her chair. "Something's going on with Max. I wonder if…well, if he's dating someone and hasn't told me."

"If he was…would it bother you?"

Jess nodded. For some reason talking about guy stuff was easier for her with her grandmother than with her dad. "I've been wanting to be more than friends for a while now."

"Does he know how you feel?"

She shrugged. "Probably."

"Don't be so sure. Men can be daft. Did I ever tell you that I was the one who asked your grandpa out on our first date?"

"Really?"

"We were part of the same group of friends in high school. I hoped he would ask me out, but when he didn't, I started dating this other guy, Craig Larson was his name. But after a few months I realized it was no good. I still liked your grandfather better."

"Was Grandpa dating anyone else?"

"No. And that gave me hope. So I broke up with Craig and waited to see if Pat would ask me out. But he didn't."

Even knowing how the story would turn out, Jess was interested. "So then what?"

"I decided there where two possibilities. Either he truly didn't care about me or he was too shy to ask me out. I'd had enough of waiting, so one night when we were at a mutual friend's party, I cornered him and asked if he'd like to go to a movie with me."

Her grandmother was blushing. She looked so cute. "Obviously he said yes."

"That's right. And as of next spring we'll have been married forty-two years." Her grandmother got out of the chair and came around the desk to give Jess a hug. "The point is, honey, you can never know for sure what's in someone else's head—or heart. I think you should tell Max how you feel."

"But what if he doesn't feel the same way?"

"Wouldn't it be better to know for sure than to torture yourself with wondering?"

LEVI WOKE EARLY on set-up day and ate breakfast alone. He was feeling down after his day out with Grace. He felt he'd handled the conversation about Costa Rica badly. Yet he was still annoyed with Grace. She hadn't even made an effort to see the situation from his point of view. House sparrows were singing madly in the hedge that bordered the courthouse when he arrived shortly after dawn. His sub-committee members were due in ten minutes. But Erin was already on site.

After they exchanged good mornings she glanced up at the blue sky. "Thank God the forecast is good for the weekend."

"We can handle rain. But it's so much easier without it," Levi agreed.

Erin was dressed in a silk blouse, skirt and blazer. She would spend most of the day in her office, handling PR and administrative matters for the event, whereas Levi—in jeans and one of his custom-lettered black T-shirts—fully expected to be on his hands and knees in the grass and dirt many times that day.

Clipboard in hand, Levi waved for his committee to gather around him. Most of the volunteers had worked with him before, and it was a straightforward matter to assign their responsibilities and let them get at it. To them fell the job of actually putting up the tents for the festival and making sure the food trucks and port-a-potties and garbage, recycling and compost bins were in their proper locations.

At noon Levi quickly checked in at the store to see how things were going.

Roy Sandhu, his assistant manager, was busy but not overwhelmed. "We're good, boss. Don't worry about things here."

Reassured, Levi returned to the park. Artists were beginning to show up now and lay claim to their spaces. The variety of products on display always amazed him. Everything from custom jewelry to hand-stitched quilts to wood carvings. Levi knew most of the artists—their wares and how they liked to display them—personally. In some ways that helped—he was able to anticipate problems before anyone complained. But it also meant he had to stop and chat for five or ten minutes before moving on to the next booth.

Eventually he worked his way to the center of the park, where Grace was unloading framed prints from a trolley. She was in faded jeans today and a long-sleeved navy T-shirt. The simple outfit was practical, but also flattering. She looked as good in her jeans now as she had as a teenager. For some reason that pissed him off, and when she started struggling with a metal contraption, he was tempted to leave her to it.

But it was his job to help.

"Hey, Grace," he said in a tone that was friendly but not overly so.

As he strode toward her, she turned and smiled. Their gazes met—briefly—and he saw a slight frown line etch into her brow. "Good morning...or I guess it's afternoon, isn't it? These darn easels can be awkward to set up."

He took the contraption from her and easily unfolded the legs, then locked them into position.

"Damn it, Levi. You didn't have to make it look that simple."

A corner of his mouth lifted in a smile that he didn't want to make. After yesterday, he thought he'd be best keeping his distance from Grace Hamilton.

"Thanks again for yesterday. I had such a great time."

So had he, and that was the problem.

"Yeah, it was a good day," he said briskly. "The Henslow's sparrow was a real highlight."

"From a birding perspective, I agree with you."

He avoided the challenging light in her eyes by opening the other four easels for her. When he was done, she carefully placed framed photographs on display.

Levi recognized all of them from her new book. "How did you pick just five? They were all so good."

"Thanks. When I first make a photograph it always feels like the most amazing work I've ever done. But over time I'm able to see them more impartially. I really do think these five are the best of the book."

Levi took his time studying each of the photographs. But the first one Grace had put up kept drawing his eye. A magpie on the back of a majestic bison, in beautiful Yellowstone National Park. The image itself was spectacular. The bison's thick winter coat sparkled with frost and you could see the gleam in the magpie's eye.

The story behind the photo was just as interesting. In her book Grace explained the symbiotic relationship between the bird who was getting food and the bison who was getting deloused. She managed to make it amusing and wonderous all at the same time.

Keeping his eyes on the image Levi asked, "So, has a date been set for your Costa Rica trip?"

"The first of November."

"November is a good time to leave New York." It had never been his favorite month. Besides being dark and dreary in this part of the world it was also the month Maggie had died. And the month Grace had sent him her final letter, the one that had ended everything. Other than Thanksgiving Levi couldn't think of one nice thing about November.

"Yes."

He waited to see if she would mention him coming along again. Told himself it was a good thing when she didn't, then lifted a box of books off the trolley and carried it inside the tent.

GRACE WAS WONDERING if she should apologize again for inviting Levi to Costa Rica—in hindsight she couldn't believe she'd been so foolishly impulsive—when she heard her name called out. She turned to see Alicia making her way across the greens carrying two take-out coffee cups. As Grace waved at her friend, Levi stepped out of the tent.

"I better go help some of the others," he said. "Good luck. Not that you'll need it. Your work is terrific."

"See you tonight at the reception?" She'd been planning to suggest they go together, but he was acting so polite and distant, she didn't.

"Yup." After a wave of his hand, he was off. Grace was still watching him when Alicia held one of the coffee cups under her nose.

"Mocha latte, special treat."

"Thanks, Alicia." Grace smiled at her friend as she accepted the beverage. After the first sip she sighed. "This is so delicious. I don't want to even think about all the calories."

"Right? I wouldn't drink these every day, but they're fun for special occasions. And today is pretty special. I'm so excited you decided to come to our festival this year. Everyone at my yoga class this morning was saying they couldn't wait to see you." Alicia glanced at the feature photographs. "These are terrific. What else did you bring?"

"A few boxes of books. Also some postcards and smaller prints of my most popular photographs."

"Well, I'm here to help, so put me to work. I've got two hours before I teach my next class."

"Thank you so much. Can you help me with this box of postcards?" She nodded at the trolley. "It's heavier than it looks."

As they lifted the box and placed it on one of the display tables Alicia said, "It was nice of Levi to stop by. I'm sorry if I chased him away."

"Don't worry. You didn't interrupt anything. He was just helping me with the easels. All business."

"Maybe he was just distracted. I imagine he's got a lot on his plate today." Alicia opened the box of books and began stacking them on the table.

"Yes, but that wasn't it." After the amazing day they'd spent together yesterday, Grace hadn't expected to get, if not a cold shoulder, then a cool one. "I think me getting that call about Costa Rica on our drive home yesterday bothered him. He mentioned the trip again today. Asked when I was leaving."

"Why would that bother him? He knows who you are. What you do."

"Yesterday I actually invited him to join me."

"You didn't!"

"The birding in Costa Rica has got to be the best in the world. I know he'd love it."

"Yeah, but planning a trip together when you've only just reconnected. Isn't that a bit much?"

"Probably," Grace admitted. Which wasn't like her. Normally she was very selective about including people on her work gigs. But she'd been under the spell of nostalgia. She'd felt almost as if she'd stepped into a time machine and gone back to the early days of loving Levi. Inviting him to Costa Rica had felt like the most natural thing in the world.

"But it doesn't matter," she continued. "Levi had a million reasons why he couldn't go."

"Work? His daughter?"

"Yes. All of which could be handled if he really wanted to. They were just excuses. The truth must be he doesn't want to go." She thought for a moment, then elaborated, "At least not with me."

Alicia looked at her worriedly. "Don't take his rejection too hard. It's easy to be impulsive when you're young. Not so easy when you have a business and a family."

Grace sighed. "Yes. Good point. Levi wasn't exactly impulsive when he was young, so I could hardly expect him to be impulsive now."

"The two of you are very different that way."

"Yes." Depressed by their conversation, Grace asked Alicia about her plans for her yoga studio and they chatted about that while they finished unloading the trolley and preparing the tent for customers. There was still an hour until the festival would open when Alicia left to teach her next class, so Grace strolled the grounds with her camera, soaking in the atmosphere.

She took pictures of little vignettes that amused her or were beautiful or touching. A chipmunk sneaking crumbs dropped by a volunteer who was on his lunch break. An old woman sitting in a quiet corner of her tent, knitting at a furious pace, oblivious to the noise and chaos around her. A child reaching out with wonder to touch a multi-colored silk scarf.

And Levi. He seemed to be everywhere at once that day. He kept showing up in her viewfinder assembling tents, hauling boxes, fiddling with electrical wires. And when she couldn't see him a part of her was always watching for him. Once when Grace looked up from photographing the gazebo, she spotted Levi just ten feet away talking into his hand-held radio.

When their gazes connected, they both froze for a few seconds. Grace couldn't breathe, couldn't move. It was like that moment in the wilds when you catch sight of something beautiful you've been tracking for ages and ages and you reach for your camera knowing this might be the only chance you get.

Only, in this case Grace didn't touch her camera.

And then Levi turned his head away from her, resumed talking on his radio, and the moment was gone.

October 4, 1999
New York University

Dear Levi,

Remember I was telling you about my *Visual Thinking* class? Our prof is so cool. He says eventually our camera will feel like a natural extension of our bodies. When he was a kid, he used to sleep with his camera, which may sound weird, but I think it's kind of awesome, too. I took my Nikon with me to the football game on Saturday and lining up my shots made me see the game in a totally different way. Which is exactly what Professor White said would happen. He says it's our job to change the perceptions of the rest of the world. Isn't that exciting? I didn't bother going to the dance after the game. I was too excited to get to the lab and see how my pictures turned out.

P.S. Have you noticed that while we text a lot every day, we always seem to say the important stuff in our letters?

Chapter Eight

G RACE HAD A basic black dress she wore to all semi-formal occasions. She could dress it up with heels and dazzling earrings. Or take it down a notch with black pumps and a statement necklace. She asked Alicia which would be more appropriate for the cocktail reception that night.

"Give them the full treatment," her friend advised. "Heels. The works."

Grace wasn't sure. She didn't want to look like someone from the big city, dressing to impress. But when she walked into the banquet room of the Cascade Hotel she saw instantly that Alicia's advice had been correct.

Men were in suits and the women were dressed for a party with salon-styled hair, glittery dresses and strappy sandals. If anything, her outfit veered to the understated.

The room itself was gorgeous with eye-catching floral bouquets featuring autumn colors. A string quartet was playing Vivaldi while waitstaff dressed in black carrying trays of champagne and tapas mingled among the guests.

Grace stood for several moments, looking for a familiar face.

She couldn't see any.

Feeling foolishly like a teenager on the sidelines at a high school dance, she searched the crowd for anyone she knew, a way to ease into the crowd. But it had been over twenty years since she'd last lived in this town and she recognized no one.

And then. Striding into the room looking totally at ease and confident, came Levi. He took in the room at a glance then walked straight toward her. On the way he acquired two glasses of champagne and handed one to her when he drew near.

"I want to apologize. I was kind of a jerk earlier today. You look fantastic by the way."

"Thank you. I'd like to apologize too. I shouldn't have been so impulsive yesterday. Sometimes, when I'm excited about a project, I don't stop to consider the impracticalities."

"Yeah. I know that about you. It wasn't fair of me to shoot you down the way I did." He nodded toward the crowd. "Recognize anyone?"

"Not at all. I feel like I'm thirteen again and the new girl at school."

"You've come a long way since then. People are hanging back because they're impressed. Come on, let's make the rounds."

With Levi at her side Grace enjoyed meeting the event's major sponsors. She did end up remembering a few of the people, but even those who were new to her were easy to talk to. It helped having Levi by her side. She could tell how much he was liked and respected by the way people's eyes lit up when he joined a group. It had been like that when they were kids too.

Eventually they crossed paths with Clara and Sam.

"Everything is perfect, don't you think?" Clara looked very pleased. "Nice choice on the string quartet, Sam."

"Thanks. I took a walk through the artist tents earlier. Impressive showing this year, Clara."

Grace gazed at them in shock. "So the two of you can be civil with one another."

"I told you they're actually good friends when there's nothing to fight about," Levi said.

Grace was about to ask where the rest of the committee members were when Erin took center stage. With microphone in hand, she welcomed everyone to the thirty-eighth annual Woodland Arts and Autumn Foliage Festival. To Grace's eye the mayor personified fall foliage in an eye-catching silk handkerchief dress of orange and gold, the colors blending perfectly with her thick auburn hair.

"Thank you all for coming," Erin continued. "And for celebrating our community and the many talented artists and craftspeople who live here."

As the crowd applauded, Grace glanced at Levi and wondered how he could not be impressed with this woman's obvious beauty. But he wasn't even looking at Erin.

"Ready for another drink?" he asked in a low voice.

She nodded.

Meanwhile Erin kept speaking. "I also want to thank the hardworking members of the festival committee, in particular my co-chair Levi Shanahan. Levi, get up here with me!"

Warm applause accompanied Levi as he gave Grace an apologetic shrug, then made his way to the stage. He accepted the mike and thanked the crowd. "I'd like to give a special call-out to Grace Hamilton from New York City. Grace and I went to high school together. Since those days she's made a career for herself in the incredibly competitive world of wildlife photography. Her latest book—focusing on the birds that inhabit our national parks—is currently on the bestsellers' lists and for good reason—it's completely captivating. So make sure you check out her tent tomorrow."

Grace was touched by the speech and the crowd's warm reaction to it.

Erin took back the mike and encouraged the crowd to enjoy the evening. "Tomorrow I hope you'll come out and support all our artists and enjoy the wonderful lineup of entertainment that's been organized by Sam Rigby. To cap off the day we'll meet at the Woodland campground for a barbecue dinner. Hope you enjoy it all and thanks again, everyone, for your support."

Grace expected Levi to rejoin her once the speech was over. But Erin linked her arm with his and led him in a different direction. She supposed there was more committee work to attend to.

She sampled some of the tapas—a coconut chicken samosa, and then a saffron-seared scallop—both of which were delicious. Eventually she ran into a friend she remembered from high school and they chatted for a while. Then Oliver James, the lawyer on the committee, handed her a drink.

"Thirsty work, socializing."

"Agreed." She took a welcome sip of the champagne.

"Interesting town, Woodland. I moved here from Manhattan three years ago and I still feel like an outsider."

"What brought you here?"

"Burn-out at work and a broken heart after a ten-year relationship ended." He shrugged and gave a self-deprecating smile. "Thought I'd move to a small town and live some sort of bucolic, idyllic life."

"And?"

"The reality wasn't as advertised. Oh, the work is good. I bought my practice from an attorney who wanted to retire and most of his clients have been happy to stay with me. But making friends has been tough. Most of the people in my age group are already married."

Oliver's difficulty finding acceptance in the small town reminded her of how she had felt as a teenager when her family moved here. Were all small towns like Woodland? Did you have to be born in one in order to be accepted?

"Personally I think this town is lucky to have you. A skilled lawyer, willing to donate his time to important community events."

"Thank you. That's kind of you to say."

"It's the truth." Grace finished her champagne then set down the glass. "Thanks again for the drink, but it's time I got home." She'd made the rounds and she wasn't going to hang around like a wallflower, hoping Levi would come back. "Will you say goodbye for me to the others?"

She was at the coat check when Levi caught up to her.

"Going already? I still owe you a drink."

"I'll take a rain check. Tomorrow's going to be a busy day."

"I shouldn't have let Erin drag me around to all the sponsors."

"You were just doing your duty as co-chair. I was fine, honestly."

"I was hoping we could talk... This event probably isn't the place. There's a bar downstairs in the lobby. We could go there."

She really wanted to say yes. Whether she was on a hike, playing a game of chess, or working a crowd, being with Levi always felt so right and natural. And she craved more of his company.

But tonight she'd been reminded of a very important fact. She might be a successful artist, but she was still an outsider when it came to Woodland. More importantly, she was still, and always would be, an outsider when it came to having a future with Levi. "I'm tired. Maybe we can talk tomorrow."

She got a small measure of satisfaction from the disappointed expression on his face as she left.

THE WOODLAND PICNIC site was booked for the town barbecue on the Saturday evening of every Foliage Festival weekend, but on Friday the teenagers of the town claimed it as their own. It had been this way for as long as Jess could remember, and her dad said it had been the same when he was young.

The ingredients for the evening were relatively simple. A massive bonfire. Hotdogs and marshmallows. And bring your own beverages, whatever they may be. Jess had hot apple cider in her insulated water bottle. Lots of her friends were into beer and other substances, but Jess trained too hard as a runner to mess with any of that.

For Jess evenings like these were one of the best things about living in Woodland. The big snapping, crackling fire pushed out an inviting heat into the cool autumn night. When the smoke got too much, all you had to do was walk down by the river's edge and perch on one of the big flat rocks.

Some of the kids even braved the frigid water for a midnight swim. Last year Jess and Max had tried it. Getting in the water had been torture. But once submerged, Jess was surprised how quickly her body adapted. And after she'd toweled off and changed into dry clothes in the public restroom, she'd felt so energized.

Tonight Jess was wearing a bikini under her fleece jacket and jeans in case Max was up for the adventure again. First she had to find him though. She'd arrived at the party late because she'd had to fill in for one of the festival volunteers in charge of decorating the town hall for the cocktail party.

Jess's job had been to haul flower arrangements from the delivery van to the tables inside the hall. A relatively easy job except people kept changing their mind about where, exactly, the flowers should be placed. By the time Jess got home to change for her own party, Max had already left, along with a group of their friends.

She'd walked here on her own, trying not to mind that he hadn't waited. But if she was honest with herself, she did mind. Ever since she'd been old enough to go, she'd always come with Max. Generally in a group with other people, so it wasn't a date. But would it have killed him to miss a few hours of the party and wait for her? Better yet, if he'd come to the hall to help her with the flowers, they both could have got here at least an hour earlier. But when she'd told him about her dad's last-minute request for help, he hadn't offered.

Jess noticed a friend of hers toasting a wiener near the fire. She grabbed a roasting stick and a marshmallow and went to stand beside her.

"Hey, Devon." They had never been close friends, but they saw each other regularly at parties. "Been here long?"

"Hey, Jess. Yeah, Zek and me helped start the fire." She shifted slightly so Jess could see the husky, blond-haired guy beside her. "You know Zek?"

Jess knew him to see him. He was the quarterback of the football team. He gave her a polite smile and she said, "Hey," before turning to Devon again. "Have you seen Max?"

"Sure. We were down by the river about twenty minutes ago. Saw him and some others dive into the swimming hole." Devon made a show of shivering. "Crazy. I bet they'll be coming to the fire soon to warm up."

Trying not to show how this news pained her, Jess gave a fleeting smile then moved away from the fire. One side of her marshmallow was charred black, the other hard and white. She popped the whole thing in her mouth, not noticing how it tasted.

He'd gone swimming already. Without her.

It felt like such a betrayal, but was it? Jess tried to see things from his point of view. It wasn't his fault Jess had agreed to help her father out with the cocktail party. And someone else had probably suggested jumping into the water, maybe even dared Max to do it.

Jess could feel her body relaxing, her mind calming down. Her father had taught her that wild emotional reactions should not be trusted. *Think things through*, he always told her if she came home upset about something that had happened at school.

She headed toward the riverbank but couldn't see Max or any of their group. Maybe they'd gone to change out of their wet swimsuits. Rather than go to the restrooms and check, Jess climbed up a big boulder, then lay back so she could see the stars. It was a clear night and with a stand of trees blocking the light from the bonfire, the sky was dazzling. She let her gaze sink into the millions—billions?—of stars making up the Milky Way. Looking at stars always made her think of her mother. She didn't know why. It was weird—and scary—to think that she had been only six years older than Jess was right now when she had died.

Suddenly Jess felt terribly lonely. She pushed herself upright, then scrambled down the rock. Max and the gang should be back by the fire by now.

Sand and small pebbles crunched under her trainers as she followed the path back to the campsite. The bonfire appeared even larger than it had earlier. Funny how she'd never noticed before that the flames were the same colors as the fall foliage that made their part of the world so famous.

She was pulling out her phone to try texting Max—though with all the noise of people talking and laughing and the music being played by a group who were dancing by the fire, she doubted he would hear it—when she spotted his familiar face. He was on the other side of the bonfire from her, talking to some girl Jess didn't recognize. The girl was pretty. And her hair was wet.

And then Jess noticed something else. The girl had her

hand on Max's arm. A moment later Max bent to say something in the girl's ear. They both laughed.

For a moment Jess felt numb, as her brain tried to reject what she had just seen. This couldn't be happening. Max belonged to her. He was her best friend. Her best everything. He should have been swimming with her. Telling his jokes to her.

But it was no good. Even after she'd turned away the image of the two of them remained burned in her mind.

She took a few tentative steps away from the fire. Her gut ached as if she'd been physically punched. She wished desperately that she was home where she could curl up in her bed and let the misery swamp her without worrying about anyone seeing her fall apart. Instead she held her head high and kept moving. When a guy she knew from cross-country said hello, she managed a smile and kept moving.

Eventually she made it to the fringe of the gathering. It was colder here. Darker. Jess had come on foot expecting to get a ride home with Max. Obviously that wasn't going to happen.

She started to sob. Then clamped her lips tight. When she was sure no one could see her anymore, Jess succumbed to her instincts. And fled.

THE NEXT MORNING Grace felt emotionally flat as she

contemplated the day ahead. Last night had been disappointing on many levels. Reminding her that she was an outsider in this town. And cementing the fact that she and Levi were simply not meant to be. Erin had used the co-chair role to manipulate Levi into spending most of the evening by her side. But Levi had allowed it to happen. So, even though he claimed not to be interested in the mayor, maybe secretly he was.

Which was fine. Their lives dovetailed perfectly. Much better than Grace and Levi's ever could.

There was a knock on the door. Then Alicia called out, "Are you decent?"

"Still in bed. But come on in."

Alicia entered with a tray containing a thermos and a plate of muffins. "Emergency caffeine intervention. You are aware the festival opens in an hour?"

Grace scrambled out of bed to help her friend with the tray. "You're so sweet. And I'm the worst guest. I should be helping you with the boys, not causing you more work."

"No sweat. Sean and the boys are watching cartoons and later his parents are coming to take the boys fishing." Alicia uncapped the thermos and poured out two cups of coffee.

"That smells heavenly." Grace accepted a mug, then joined Alicia on the slipcovered sofa beside the small table where she'd put the tray.

"I didn't hear you come in last night," Alicia said. "Did you stay late?"

"Not really. I made the rounds and then decided to call it a night."

"Did you spend much time with Levi?"

"I couldn't. Your mayor was clinging to Levi like they were co-joined as well as co-chairs."

"Are you terribly disappointed? I know you thought maybe you and Levi…"

Grace shook her head. "We wanted different things when we were young, and we still want different things." She shrugged. It all sounded so logical. So cut and dried. "If only I didn't still want him so much."

"It must be hard. But you're going to be so busy you won't have a chance to miss him or anyone else. And I'll be there to help you."

"Are you sure? You've been such a help already. And Sean is probably hoping to get some alone time with you."

"Honestly? He'd love to have a day free to work on his next project—a tree house for the kids. When they're around they insist on helping and it ends up taking him three times as long."

"Well then, I accept your kind offer. At least we'll be able to visit during all the slow times."

BUT IT TURNED out Alicia was right. There were no slow times. From the moment Grace opened her tent for business, she was swamped with people coming to admire her work. Most bought a little something, a bookmark or a few post-cards. She sold a respectable number of her books and prints as well.

True to her word, Alicia was a great help. She handled payments and wrote out receipts for cash purchases and when it became clear that Grace wouldn't have time for lunch, grabbed her a smoothie.

While Alicia was gone, a familiar-looking teenager stopped by the tent to say hello.

"So you came," Rae Stedwell said.

"Thanks to you putting the idea in my head. It's been...an experience. How did you do on your school project?"

Rae glanced over her shoulder before answering. "Oh, I, um, I got an A plus. Thanks again for helping me."

"It was a pleasure."

"Okay. Well. I just wanted to say hi. I can see you're really busy."

Grace would have tried to engage her for longer, but it was true there were others in the tent trying to get her attention.

As the day wore on Grace was touched by the number of older people who wanted to say hi because they had known her parents. She made a list of the names so she could remember them to her mom and dad next time she called.

A lot of old classmates came by, too, as well as friends

from her neighborhood. At four o'clock—scheduled closing time—the crowds began clearing. Grace realized there was one person she'd been hoping would stop by but hadn't.

Levi. Every now and then she caught sight of him in the crowd. If he wasn't talking to someone, he was moving purposefully as if on the way to solve one problem or another. She got that he was busy. But she'd thought he would have found time to at least stop in and say hi.

JESS HAD AVOIDED her father at breakfast and spent most of Saturday morning in her room. Around noon she went to the festival, driven by guilt, to say hello to Grace Hamilton. She cut her visit short, afraid someone she knew would come by and call her by name. Back in her room she felt more miserable than ever. Around two o'clock she heard a small stone hit the side of the house, close to her window. She pulled up the blind and opened the window.

Max was on the lawn, his hands on his hips. "Ready to head to the festival?"

"I've already been."

"So come again."

"Nah."

"Hang on. I'm coming inside." Max disappeared from view and a second later Jess heard their front door open. She let out a heavy sigh then left her room.

Jess met him in the hallway. She hung back, keeping several feet between them. "I mean it Max. I'm not going."

He pulled at his thick hair, agitated. "What happened to you last night? Did you get stuck at your dad's event until late?"

She took a deep breath. "I showed up at the bonfire around eight thirty. Tried to find you guys, then I heard you'd already gone swimming."

She firmed her jaw and glared at him. Challenging him to admit he'd stood her up.

But he refused to admit he'd done anything wrong.

"You should have waited for us by the fire. Didn't you figure we'd need to warm up?"

"I did wait by the fire. And I did see you. But you were with some girl."

"That doesn't sound..." His eyes widened. "Oh, you must mean Lexi. We did talk for a bit."

Jealousy and suspicion swirled in Jess. She'd never felt this way before and she hated it. She wanted to turn and run, just like she'd done last night.

But then her grandmother's advice came back to her. *Just ask.*

Jess swallowed. Then took a deep breath. "Are you going out with her?"

"What?"

She'd been hoping for an answer of "no" not "what." The anger in his voice threw her off-balance. "You never come over in the evenings anymore."

"So...what...you think I've been going out with some girl?"

Suddenly she felt utterly miserable. She'd never known Max to be so angry and confrontational. If only she hadn't said anything. But it was too late for that. Since he was already mad she might as well find out the worst. "Is it Lexi...?"

"Damn it, Jess."

He looked at her like she'd just betrayed him, when in fact it was probably the other way around. Not that she had any romantic claim to him. But as friends—best friends—he ought to have told her.

"Sure. I'm dating another girl. In fact, I'm dating more than one girl. Is that okay with you?"

She would not let him see she was upset. "Whatever."

He glared at her, then stormed off. For several minutes she stared at the door he had slammed, practically in her face.

She and Max had had fights before. But never, never like this.

October 12, 1999
New York University

Dear Levi,

I get what you're saying about the college experience being about more than studying. But when I'm making pictures it never feels like work. Everything else—especially the parties and social events you think I should be taking part in—all seem so lame. And I have made some friends, a couple kids from my Visual Thinking class. We're planning to go gallery hopping in the city again next weekend. By the way, it's been a while since you sent me any of your sketches. What (or who) is keeping you so busy over there?

Chapter Nine

F ESTIVAL DAY WENT by in a blur for Levi and then
suddenly it was tear-down time. When he was younger
Levi had been one of the guys bringing down the tents,
doing the heavy lifting. Now he got to supervise, trouble-
shoot and lend a hand when necessary. He and his team had
two hours before the barbecue began and he intended they
would leave the park as pristine as they had found it.

After checking on the team dismantling the sound
equipment at the gazebo, he headed to Grace's tent. All her
framed prints had sold and she was trying to fold up the
easels.

"Let me help you with that."

She stepped back to give him space. "Thanks." A few
strands of her blond hair had worked loose from the knot at
the nape of her neck and there were wrinkles in her sand-
colored linen pants, but other than that she seemed unfazed
by her busy day.

"Looks like you were a big success. I came by a few times
to see how you were doing, but there was always a lineup."

"Really? I never saw you."

She seemed a bit cool. Was it about today? Or last night? "Sorry again about last night. I shouldn't have let Erin drag me around like that."

"No need to apologize. I didn't need a babysitter."

"That wasn't what I meant. I was just sorry we didn't get a chance to talk more. Erin's been making way too much of this co-chair business."

"Maybe because she likes you?"

Levi's ears were suddenly too warm. He looked away for a moment, then shook his head. "Maybe she does. I'm not sure why. We don't have much in common."

"You have Woodland in common," Grace pointed out.

Something he and Grace did not. "Touché." He picked the last of her boxes from the ground and added it to the trolley. "Can I make last night up to you and escort you to the barbecue?"

"No need. I have my own car."

"I do realize you are capable of getting to the barbecue on your own. I just thought it would be nice to go together."

"I'm not sure that's a good idea."

He took a deep breath. "Are you upset because I turned down Costa Rica? Look, I'm sorry but it's just not possible for me."

"No need to apologize. We haven't seen each other in twenty years and suddenly I'm asking you to come to Costa Rica with me. Crazy, right? I was just pumped after our great day together—"

"It was a great day," Levi agreed. "It's been nice having you back in Woodland. You'll be leaving soon and I figure the barbecue will be like my last chance to spend some time with you."

"I guess we would save gas if we carpooled."

He laughed. "We'll be driving one mile so we ought to save at least a quarter."

"Totally worth it."

"I'll pick you up at seven."

"YOU SURE YOU don't want to come with us?" Alicia was at the door to the guesthouse, looking elegant in the black silk pantsuit she'd bought in New York. And mildly worried.

Grace shook her head. "Thanks but Levi just texted me. He's almost here. I'll catch up with you and Sean and the boys once we get there."

Alicia narrowed her eyes. She started to say something. Stopped. And then smiled. "That's a pretty dress."

"Thank you." Grace executed a pirouette. Her soft cotton dress had a small floral print and a flowing skirt. For warmth she was teaming it with boots, a denim jacket, and a soft, scrunchy scarf. "For the record, you look absolutely stunning."

"The family's in the truck waiting for me. So...you're sure you're okay?"

Grace nodded. Despite her better judgment she felt an almost giddy sense of anticipation. Tonight she would not think about her inevitable departure from Woodland or Levi's refusal of her offer to travel to Costa Rica. She would just enjoy his company.

"Okay then," Alicia said. "I'll see you there." She had almost closed the door when she opened it again. "Levi just drove up."

"Thanks. Tell him I'll be right there." Grace slipped her cell phone into her camera case, then slung the strap over her shoulder. Levi was already out of his truck when she made it to the street. She waved to Alicia and her family as they drove off, then turned to Levi.

In dark jeans and a nicely tailored blue shirt he looked amazing. The way he was smiling at her told her he had the same opinion of her. For a moment she felt eighteen again, desperate for the boy she loved to kiss her.

Then she flashed forward twenty years. And there was no kiss. All Levi did was open the passenger door.

As she settled into her seat, her younger self re-emerged. When you were a teenager, a vehicle equaled freedom and she and Levi had sought the open road at every opportunity. She felt that same sense of heady opportunity now. Secretly she prayed for him to head for the open highway. But of course he didn't. In just ten minutes they were at the barbecue.

She unfastened her seat belt, then looked over at Levi. "I

hope I'm finally going to be able to meet Jessica tonight."

Levi's smile faltered. "Afraid not. She's going to hang out with her grandfather tonight."

"Your parents aren't going to the barbecue either?" Grace couldn't help feeling relieved. She'd gotten along fine with Levi's father when she was dating Levi, but his mother had always been a touch cool. Levi claimed she was imagining things. He told her his mother liked her just fine. But Grace's instincts said otherwise.

"Mom will be there but Dad hasn't been very social since he was diagnosed with atherosclerosis."

"Is that when your arteries have plaque buildup?" When Levi nodded, she asked, "Is he going to require surgery?"

"Maybe in the future. For now he's being asked to watch his diet and avoid strenuous activities."

"Well it's nice of your daughter to keep him company. Not many teenagers would give up a Saturday night like that."

"Jess wouldn't normally either." Levi sounded worried. "Something's been off with her the last little while. I feel guilty—I've been so busy I haven't been around much."

"She'll talk to you when she's ready."

"I hope so."

The sun had set a short while ago and it was dusk as they left the truck, walking side by side, their arms occasionally jostling against each other.

When they rounded the curve to the clearing by the river, Grace paused to take it all in. The picnic shelter was outlined in lights and a big tent had been erected for the five-piece band, currently playing "Sweet Home Alabama." Already a group was gathered, dancing, while yet more people were lined up for pulled pork sandwiches and salads.

"Wow, impressive. I remembered the barbecue being more casual."

"It was more like a potluck picnic when we were young," Levi said. "Now we hire a caterer with a big commercial barbecue. About ten years ago we added the band and the dancing. In about an hour, when it's fully dark, there'll be fireworks."

As she automatically reached for her camera, Grace missed a small rock on the path and stumbled.

"Careful," Levi said.

There were fireworks already, Grace thought, when Levi put his arm around her waist to steady her.

Levi waited patiently as she lined up a few shots. Then, as they moved into the crowd, she heard someone call out his name. Not ready to share him with the rest of the town just yet, she reached for his hand. "How about we start things off with a dance?"

Last time she'd danced with Levi had been at an outdoor party with friends, the night before she left for college. He'd held her close while Toni Braxton sang "Unbreak my heart," and neither one of them had realized that in just a few months, they would be the ones with the hearts needing to be unbroken.

"Excellent idea." Levi's hand around her waist tightened as he led her toward the dance area. Most couples were dancing separately but as the band transitioned to "Where The Sidewalk Ends," Levi swung her into a two-step.

She couldn't believe how naturally they moved together, even after all this time.

The song ended and another began, but Grace was oblivious to the words and the tune. All she noticed was Levi pulling her in closer for a waltz. She let her head rest against his shoulder and inhaled the warm, male scent of him.

How could it be that after all these years she still felt like she belonged in his arms? She closed her eyes, hoping for the moment to go on and on, but all too soon someone shouted out Levi's name, too loudly, this time, to be ignored. Levi stopped moving and Grace peered over her shoulder.

Oliver was waving at them from the edge of the dance area. "Hey, Levi, isn't your phone working? Erin wants all the committee members to meet by the picnic tables for a few minutes.

"Damn," Levi said softly. He took one of Grace's hands. "Come with me? I don't want to lose you in the crowd."

"You won't. I'll join the drinks lineup. Come find me when you're ready."

"I won't be long."

Within a few seconds he had disappeared into the crowd while Grace headed in the opposite direction, to the lineup for beverage tickets. Just her luck, Mary Shanahan was in the lineup ahead of her. She greeted Grace with a glacial smile.

Grace's answering smile felt far from natural. "Hi, Mrs. Shanahan, it's nice to see you again."

"Hi, Grace. Pat and I sure were surprised when we heard you were coming to the festival this year."

Good surprised or bad surprised, Grace wanted to ask, even though she thought she knew the answer. "The timing happened to work for me this year."

"How fortunate." Mary paused then added, "I meant to drop by your booth today, but every time I tried you had a big crowd."

"Everyone's been very supportive. I didn't expect so many people to remember me and my parents."

"Even though you only lived in Woodland a short while, people here are proud of you. You've done good, Grace."

"Thank you." The last thing she'd expected from Levi's mother was a compliment. And it sounded genuine. Grace started to relax, but Mary wasn't finished.

"I always saw that possibility for greatness in you. Even when you were a teenager. It takes more than talent. A person has to have a hunger, a passion. You had that."

"Yes, I suppose I did."

"I knew you'd never come back to Woodland after college. And I worried about Levi. Now, after seeing the two of you dancing together, I can't help worrying again." Mary stopped. Shook her head. "I'm not sure my son is thinking straight. I don't think he ever could where you were concerned."

"What, exactly, is your point, Mary?"

"My boy lost his wife so young and he's spent the past eighteen years raising his daughter. I want him to find happiness again...not get his heart broke one more time."

Grace lost her words, lost her very breath. She'd always suspected Mary didn't like her. But this warning hammered home the point.

Finally Grace drew a breath. "I'm sorry about Levi's wife. But that loss had nothing to do with me. Why do you assume I'm going to break his heart?"

"What else are you going to do? You were born to wander, Grace. And Levi—he's as rooted to this place as a mighty oak tree." She paused and then admitted, "Still, it's not my place to interfere. Levi's going to be good and mad at me. I guess he has that right. As do you. But sometimes a mother can't stop herself."

Mary stepped forward then, to buy her drinks tickets. Completely discombobulated, Grace slipped out of the lineup and moved aimlessly through the crowd. Everyone around her continued to laugh and talk and mingle. Was it possible they hadn't heard any of the exchange? Grace searched the crowd desperately for a friendly face and almost cried out when she spotted Alicia. Her friend had two tall paper cups in her hands and was walking toward her.

"You okay? I saw you talking to Mary Shanahan and you

got awfully pale." Alicia passed her one of the cups. "Spiced apple cider. It's very tasty."

"Thank you." Grace hadn't realized how dry her throat was. She took several gulps of the sweet, flavorful beverage. "Wait until you hear what Mary said to me."

"Tell me."

Alicia led her to a park bench away from the action. It was cooler here, but thanks to the rising full moon and clear skies, there was ample light. Grace felt her heart rate calm. "This is nice. Thanks. It helps to get away from the crowd for a bit."

"So what happened?"

As she recounted her conversation with Mary, Grace expected Alicia to speak up with supportive indignation. But she remained quiet and finally Grace had to prod. "Tell me you agree that Mary went way over the line."

"She did," Alicia said. "But I suppose she's just worried what will happen to Levi once you return to Manhattan or go traveling on your next assignment."

Grace pulled back. "My heart is on the line here, too. Not just Levi's."

"Exactly. Which is why I'm worried too. You deserve to be loved by someone who can give you everything you need. Is Levi that guy?"

But I love him.

Grace knew better than to say the words out loud. Love hadn't been enough the first time. What made her think it would be the second? If Levi couldn't even commit to a three-week trip to Costa Rica with her, how could they possibly have a future?

"I don't think logically when I'm around him," she admitted. "I think it's time I went back to Manhattan."

"That might be for the best."

Grace knew her friendship with Alicia would survive this moment. But right now she felt betrayed. She wanted Alicia to take her side against Mary, to tell her she should stay and fight for the man she loved. But maybe that was what real friends did. Made you face the truth, even when it was painful.

"I'll go back to your place to pack. Okay if I leave the key under the doormat?"

"You're going to leave right now? Tonight?"

Grace nodded. Clean and fast breaks were always the easiest.

"Let me grab the keys from Sean and I'll drive you home and help you pack."

"No. I'd like to walk. By myself. I need to clear my head."

"It's too far to go in the dark."

"You and I walked that path in the night a hundred times when we were young. Besides—" Grace unzipped her camera case to display the contents. "I'm used to getting caught out in the wilderness after dark. I always travel with a headlamp. And Mace. I'll be fine."

October 21, 1999
New York University

Dear Levi,

I'll never think your sketches are silly and childish. I can't believe you even said that. And my new friends' names are Matt and Ethan. As for last Saturday, I didn't just have a good time. I saw a show that changed my life! Frans Lanting is a Dutch nature and wildlife photographer and the show we went to was called "Jungles" and the pictures he makes are like nothing I've ever seen or imagined was possible. And he doesn't just make amazing pictures. He tells stories, just like you said I should do with mine.

I began this year not sure if I wanted to be a studio photographer like my dad, or what. But after seeing Frans Lanting's work, I know. I want to go where the wild creatures are. Not just here in America, but all over the world! I want to find my own unique perspective and tell my own stories about what I see. The possibilities feel endless to me right now and all I wish was that you were here...to hold my hand and dream with me.

Chapter Ten

LEVI FOLLOWED OLIVER to the picnic table where Erin, Sam and Clara were enjoying a celebratory drink. Clara passed them each a plastic tumbler of wine.

"Not a single glitch. Well done, team." Erin high-fived every one of the committee members.

Levi grinned. He was damn pleased with all of them, too. "I've been on this committee for over a decade and this was our smoothest year yet."

"We had great leadership." Sam clinked his plastic wineglass against Levi's and then Erin's. "You two make a good team."

"I give a lot of that credit to Erin." Levi gave her a mock bow. "Considering it was your first year on the committee you were amazing. You hit the ground running from the first day. And much as I complained about your social media accounts, they sure were effective at drawing a crowd."

"If I did well, it's because I had great mentorship," Erin demurred.

Clara looked from Erin to Levi. "Like Sam said, you two make a good team. Maybe you all should find another project you could work on together." She punctuated this with a heavy-handed wink.

"Such as?" Levi suspected the older committee members were up to a little matchmaking and this conclusion was supported when they both got up from the picnic table pulling Oliver along with them.

"We'll leave you two alone so you can discuss the possibilities," Sam said.

Once they were gone Levi turned to Erin who responded by covering her face with her hands.

"Ugh. The embarrassment. I feel like I'm in high school and someone just told a boy that I liked him."

Did Erin like him that way? Levi hoped not. "Don't be embarrassed. It's the peril of being single. Everyone assumes you won't be happy until they find someone to pair you up with. How long do you think Sam and Clara have been hatching this plan?"

"Pretty much since Clara suggested you invite me to co-chair the committee." Erin let out a long sigh, then topped up both their wineglasses. "I knew she was hoping something romantic would happen between the two of us. And to be honest, after my awful breakup, I was open to the idea."

Now it was Levi's turn to be embarrassed. "I, um, do like you Erin, of course I do, but, um…"

"Don't worry." Erin patted his hand. "I saw you dancing with Grace. It's pretty obvious how you feel about her."

Levi was relieved that he didn't have to explain further.

"So this matchmaking endeavor…how many folks were in on it?"

"The idea originated with your mother's coffee group. They were the ones who suggested Clara invite me to the committee. And your assistant manager at the store gave his thumbs-up as well."

"Roy too? Sounds like all this scheming happened right under my nose."

"Apparently the only one who didn't seem excited about the idea was the woman who works behind your food counter…Connie Wilson."

"Connie and I—and Grace—went to school together."

"So you're old friends. Was there ever more to it?"

"Connie and me? Nope." At least not on his part. Shortly after his breakup with Grace, it had seemed Connie was encouraging him. He'd made a point not to be alone with her once he guessed how she was feeling. Then, he'd met Maggie and the rest was history.

"Well, I'm glad we've cleared the air," Erin said. "I hope we can still be friends?"

"Of course."

"And you'll co-chair the festival committee with me again?"

"Not on your life."

She laughed. "Well, it was worth a try. I guess I'll—"

The rest of her comment was cut off when Oliver stepped forward resolutely from the crowd and walked up to her. "Would you like to dance?"

Surprise was replaced with a pleased sort of speculation in Erin's eyes. She accepted Oliver's proffered hand.

"Excuse us, Levi," Oliver said politely.

"Have fun." Levi checked his watch. Damn. More than twenty minutes had passed since he'd left Grace at the drinks lineup. He'd never find her again with all these people. He got out his phone to send a text. *Where are you?*

As he waited for her reply, he tried to make his way through the crowd, but people kept stopping him to congratulate him on the success of the festival. Finally he bumped into Alicia. She was in a group, but when he motioned, she excused herself and joined him.

"What's up, Levi?"

"It's Grace. I've lost her in the crowd. And she's not answering my text messages."

Alicia hesitated, then said, "She decided to go home."

"Home as in your place?"

"No. Manhattan."

"What—tonight?"

Alicia nodded.

"I don't get it. She was looking forward to the barbecue. We were going to—" Levi stopped himself. The details of their plans didn't matter now. "Did something happen to upset her?"

Alicia's gaze shifted to a picnic table about twenty feet away where his mother was sitting, watching them. His mom averted her face when he caught her eye. And then he knew.

"My mother said something to Grace, didn't she?"

Alicia looked torn. "They did have a conversation, yes."

"About me?"

"I—yes."

"I can't believe this." Levi couldn't remember ever being so angry with his mother. "I'm a grown man for God's sake." He would have this out with his mother eventually. But he was losing time here.

"Don't be too upset with her." Alicia touched his arm entreatingly. "All your mom wants is to protect you. Also…its partly my fault too. When Grace told me what happened…I kind of defended your mom."

"How did Grace leave? I drove her here. She doesn't have her car."

"She's walking back to my house."

Levi was incredulous. "In the dark? Alone?"

"I didn't like the idea either. But she insisted she knew the route and she had a headlamp and Mace with her…not that she's likely to need either."

"How long ago did she leave?"

Alicia consulted her watch. "About ten minutes or so."

"Okay. Thanks." He strode through the crowd, this time brushing off anyone who wanted to talk with a curt, "Sorry."

Once out of the crush of people, Levi broke into a trot and soon he was beyond the reach of artificial light. With moonlight guiding him he joined the river path where he was finally able to break out into a run. It felt good to channel his anxiety into action. To know every stride was taking him closer. With her boots, Grace would only be able to walk. He'd catch her before long.

And yet, it seemed he was running for a long time. His lungs began to burn. His legs felt ten pounds heavier than normal. He'd thought all his hiking was keeping him in shape but apparently he'd been kidding himself.

His breathing was loud and heavy in his ears, but above that he could hear twigs and leaves snapping and crunching underfoot. The haunting call of a great horned owl made him pause for a second, but then he pushed on, even faster than before.

And then he saw her. Just a figure up ahead at first. As he narrowed the gap he could see the swishing of her full skirt, the gleam of her blond hair in the moonlight.

"Grace." He was so out of breath he could hardly get her name out. But it was enough to make her stop. Turn around.

"Is that you, Levi?"

He was close enough now to see her eye makeup had smeared and the tip of her nose was red. She wasn't crying now. But she had been.

He walked up beside her and took her hand. "Why are you leaving? What's wrong?"

"I just realized I don't belong here. I'm not sure I ever did."

"I'm confused. Just a few hours ago you told me how

overwhelmed you were by the support you'd been given by our community."

"I think they do support me as an artist. But not—" She stopped and redirected. "Let's just say that arriving at the barbecue with you was not a smart move."

"I thought it was an excellent move." He tugged her closer. "I hope this isn't about something my mother said to you. I love my mom, but she has no business interfering in my life or our relationship."

"She was only saying what everyone else in town—even my best friend—thinks. That a relationship between you and me is doomed to fail." Grace pulled her hands from his. "It's no good, Levi. I should just go home. Back to Manhattan. That's where I belong now. Not here."

Blood pounded in Levi's head. He didn't want her to go. Definitely not like this. "It's only seven thirty. Come back to my house. We'll have a cup of coffee and talk this through."

She tilted her head, as she considered the idea.

"It's a three-hour drive back to Manhattan. Doesn't it make sense to have a coffee and a chance to calm down before you get behind the wheel?"

"I suppose. But I'll tell you right now, you won't change my mind about leaving."

Maybe not. But he had to try.

GRACE PAUSED ON the front porch of Levi's house. The cushioned wicker chairs, pumpkins and potted flowers made for a welcoming entrance. You'd never guess a single dad was running this household. But Levi was not your average single dad.

Turn and run home, her inner voice beseeched her. Leaving Woodland and Levi was only going to get harder if she stepped inside this house. But after he unlocked the door and motioned her inside, she went.

"Jess, you home?" Levi called out. When there was no answer, he turned to Grace. "Maybe she's still at my dad's. Make yourself comfortable. The kitchen is that way." He gestured to the right. "I'm going upstairs to check if Jess is in her room."

After removing her boots, Grace hung back in the hallway. As she'd feared this place was pulling on her. From the braided rug on the floor, to the warm caramel color on the walls, to the art, the ambience was of home and hearth, of comfort and acceptance.

None of these adjectives could be applied to her flat in Manhattan, which was more about light and air and space. Things she loved, Grace reminded herself. Not everyone belonged in small-town America. Hadn't that been made abundantly clear this evening?

She stepped forward to study the art. Four framed watercolors of birds had been grouped together on the wall next to the closet. Up close the details were exquisite. In the bottom left corners, she could make out a faint "*L.S.*" from the artist. She stepped back as she heard Levi running back down the stairs.

"No luck," he said. "I just sent her a text and apparently she's sleeping over at my parents' place. Now let me make you that coffee."

Grace resisted his effort to corral her into the kitchen. "These paintings. Did you make them?"

"Yeah. Amateur efforts, but Maggie liked them. She had them framed and put them up. Been there so long I don't even notice them anymore."

"I knew you sketched birds. When did you take up watercolors?"

He folded his arms over his chest. "Shortly after Jess was born."

He seemed embarrassed by her interest, but Grace couldn't stop from gushing. "These are hardly amateur. The colors, the textures, the details…everything is so incredibly accurate. And beautiful. I swear I can almost feel the fluffy down on the bluebird's plump little belly. And that sweet upper mandible. It gives him such a friendly appearance."

"If you like it so much, you're welcome to have it."

"Oh, I couldn't break up the collection." Besides the bluebird, Levi had painted a goldfinch, a golden-crowned kinglet and a red-eyed vireo, all in a similar style.

"Don't worry about it. I have a box of these in storage." He removed the bluebird and propped it next to her boots so she wouldn't forget it.

"Thank you. I have a special love for the little bluebird."

"I remember."

As she gazed into his eyes Grace felt the years fall away again. This man had been her first lover, her partner in so many wonderful adventures. Alicia was her best girlfriend, but the things she'd shared with Levi had been the most intimate and personal she'd ever shared with anyone.

And when he said that he remembered, she knew he was referring to all of it. Her favorite bird was the least of it. Levi knew where she liked to be kissed and touched, what made her cry, how to make her laugh.

She'd thought this sense of connection would have faded over time, but it hadn't.

His eyes burned into hers. She could tell he wanted to kiss her. And she wanted that too.

But Mary's warning—and Alicia's—were still too fresh. She took a deep breath. "Coffee?"

A second passed, and then another, before Levi broke his gaze. "Yes. Coming right up."

She followed him into the kitchen, a warm, inviting place with honey-colored, shaker-styled cabinets and butcher-block counters. Levi gestured for her to sit at the table while he ground coffee and put a kettle to boil.

Levi moved around his kitchen with the same relaxed ease he did everything. That was one of the many things she admired about him. No matter the circumstances—

including preparing coffee for an ex-lover—he was never flustered.

"Remember the time we ran into that female black bear and her cub at Algonquin Park?" she asked. They had been on a post-graduation camping expedition that extended all the way to Ontario, Canada. Encountering the bear and her cub had been a memorable highlight.

Levi paused in the middle of measuring coffee into the French press. "You were upset you didn't get any pictures."

"That was later. In the moment I never even thought about my camera. I was so scared, if you hadn't stayed so calm, I would have run away screaming." Which would have been the wrong thing to do. Running might have incited the bear to give chase.

Levi had known this. He'd put his arm around Grace and spoken calmly to the bear. "We're going to back up and leave you and your cub in peace. No need to get worked up."

His message had been for Grace. The sound of his voice—firm and steady—had been for the bear.

And it had worked out exactly as Levi had said it would. The bear had watched quietly as they retreated, then turned back to foraging for plant roots and insects.

"Do you still feel scared when you run into bears?" Levi asked.

"Not as long as they're not too close. Thanks to you I know how to react now. I've even become so calm that once I've retreated to a safe distance, I've been able to get some wonderful pictures of both black bears and grizzlies."

"You have," Levi said. "I especially love the one of the three cubs in your newest book."

"Thank you." She had commercial success and critical acclaim, but nothing felt as good as Levi's approval.

The kettle boiled and Levi added the water to the French press. She focused on his hands as he carried two mugs and the coffee to the kitchen table. They were strong and capable, but also elegant, with the long, nimble fingers of an artist.

She brought her mind back to their conversation. "No matter how often I encounter a bear in the wilderness, I'm always reminded of that first time. With you."

Levi let her words hang in the air for several long seconds before he answered. "We had a lot of memorable firsts." His eyes were kind and loving as he reached for her hand. "Like in the back of my truck cuddled up in our sleeping blankets."

"I wondered if you would go there."

"Damn right I would. One of my favorite memories. Definitely better than the bear one."

"Agreed." His hand felt so warm and protective over hers. At that moment she wanted two things. To sit here with him forever. And to be back in that old truck of his, exploring each other's bodies.

"Tell me," he said, still holding her hand. "Why are you in such a hurry to go back to Manhattan? I was hoping you'd stay a while longer. You owe me a chess rematch. We could get out for some more hikes. You could come here for dinner. I'd like you to meet my daughter." He frowned, slightly. "She isn't usually so elusive."

"That sounds tempting, it really does." She slipped her hand out from under his. "But at some point, I'll have to go back to Manhattan. And then to Costa Rica. And after that there'll be another trip. There always is." That was her life and right now it felt like an albatross, but Grace knew she couldn't give it up.

Levi looked troubled. "Do we have to plan out the future? Couldn't we just take this week?"

Grace wanted to say yes. More than anything she longed to prolong her time with Levi. But Levi's mother, Alicia— hell, probably half the town. Everyone seemed to think that Grace had the ability to break Levi's heart.

None seemed to worry about him breaking hers though.

"We could take this week," she agreed. "But wouldn't that make it even harder to say goodbye?"

Levi let out a long breath. He looked like he wanted to argue the point. But eventually he just said, "So...driving to the city?"

She nodded. "Driving to the city."

"We better load you with caffeine then." He plunged the French press and poured out the coffee. "Careful, it's still hot." He took a sip, then remembered. "You take milk. Let me—"

"I've got it." She was already on her feet, making her way to the fridge on the far side of the kitchen. She was about to open the door when she noticed the photos. At least a dozen were affixed to the fridge door. Grace recognized Levi, his parents, and a pretty woman she assumed was Levi's deceased wife Maggie. But the person who most snagged her interest was the girl—Levi's daughter. She was a baby in her mother's arms in one photograph, an awkward pre-teen with braces being hugged by her grandparents in another. In a more recent photo she had bloomed into a lovely young woman with honey-colored hair and Levi's thickly lashed gray eyes.

Grace leaned closer for a better look. Those eyes. How had she not realized right away?

"Is something wrong?" Levi asked.

"Your daughter...she's very beautiful." Another picture caught Grace's attention. This one included a tall and very skinny young man with thick, unruly black hair. The very same young man who had accompanied "Rae Stedwell" on her trip to Manhattan to interview Grace.

It was taking a while to sink in.

Rae Stedwell was actually Levi's daughter Jessica.

This must explain why Levi's daughter was being so un-characteristically elusive. She didn't want Grace to find out who she really was.

But why had she encouraged Grace to attend the Wood-land Autumn Foliage Festival in the first place? Had she been trying to stir up trouble? Or—could this even be possible—

doing a little matchmaking?

Whatever Jessica's motives, she clearly hadn't told her father any of it. And Grace decided, in that instant, she wouldn't either.

October 30, 1999
New York University

Dear Levi,

Thank you for the beautiful ink drawing of the campus pigeons. That's so sweet that you sneak extra toast at breakfast so you can feed them.

I'm not surprised you keep falling asleep in your econ class. I bet you wouldn't fall asleep if you were studying something you were actually interested in, like art or biology. I know you feel lucky to have a family business to inherit. And you love Woodland. But there is so much to see and do in this world.

Maybe instead of spending Thanksgiving with your folks, we should spend it here in the city? I'd love to take you to the Frans Lanting show. And to the Guggenheim. And birding in Central Park. We could have so much fun! What do you say?

Chapter Eleven

L EVI DIDN'T KNOW if it was the coffee or his emotions that were burning the hole in his gut. His every instinct was to hold on to Grace, to keep her in Woodland, to make her see they belonged together. But she was going to leave.

He couldn't argue with her logic for not staying. A week together might be fantastic, but it definitely would make it harder to say goodbye. And if this week had taught him anything, it was that his daughter still needed him. He'd been so preoccupied with the festival—and Grace—he hadn't been here for her. And that made him feel awful.

After Maggie's accident, he'd stood at her deathbed in the hospital and promised he would look after their child. He'd promised he would keep Maggie's memory alive for her and that he would always put Jessica first.

Up until this week Levi believed he'd lived up to that promise. But there was no denying that Grace had distracted him.

Was distracting him now.

He wished she'd come back to the table and continue their conversation, but she was looking at the family photos on his fridge with an almost excessive interest. He supposed it was because she'd never met Jess.

"Almost every year I add a picture to the collection. Jess teases me that I'm going to run out of fridge door soon."

Grace came back to the table with the carton of milk. She added some to her coffee, then asked, "This is probably a silly question, but does Jess know about me? That you and I used to date when we were in high school."

"It's funny you ask that. Because the subject did come up, about three weeks ago. Jess asked me about any girl-friends I had before her mother."

"That is...funny." Grace stirred her coffee, her expression pensive.

"She seemed pleased when she heard you were coming to the festival. Which is why I'm surprised she hasn't been around to meet you."

"It's curious, isn't it..."

"I can only guess she's having problems with her friend Max and she's not thinking about anything else. Teenagers can be a little self-centered." Levi paused to reflect. "It's crazy how fast it all happens. One minute you're changing diapers. The next, your kid is leaving for college."

Grace took a sip of her coffee, then smiled. "She hasn't left yet."

"No. We still have this year." And though he'd slipped up a bit the past few weeks, he still intended to make the most of this final time.

Grace took another sip of coffee. "And you'll really be okay if college inspires her to go in a different direction than Woodland and the general store? Lots of things could happen. She could develop a passion for, say, journalism. Or fall in love with a guy who wants to live in Texas."

Levi didn't know whether to laugh or groan. "That's every parent's dilemma I guess. You hope your kids end up settling somewhere close to home. But you can't clip their wings. Their happiness and fulfillment has to be the ultimate goal."

"Said the man who is the perfect father. Not every parent is so evolved in their thinking."

There was a note of bitterness in her voice. "Are you thinking of any parents in particular when you say that?"

"I probably shouldn't say this, but after seeing your paintings, I can't help feeling upset that you weren't allowed to pursue your interest in the arts."

"It wasn't that my parents didn't allow that. It just never came up." He felt honor-bound to defend his parents. However, Grace had a point. Neither of his parents had let him know he had options, which was why he was so determined not to make that mistake with Jessica.

"So you never wonder what would have happened if you'd come to college in New York with me and studied the arts?"

"I still probably would have ended up running the general store and sketching and painting as a hobby." And if this wasn't entirely true, what did it matter? Every decision he'd made that had led to Jessica being born was a decision he couldn't regret. And giving up Grace...well, that one was in her court. Even if he'd followed her to New York, they'd probably have broken up.

He noticed Grace's cup was empty. "More coffee?"

"I should get going." She took her mug to the sink and rinsed it out.

The burning sensation in his gut got worse. As he walked her to the door, he told himself it would go away soon. A few weeks from now he'd forget all about Grace Hamilton and her brief reappearance in his life.

Once she'd put on her boots he picked up the painting of the bluebird. "I'll carry this out for you."

It wasn't so big or heavy that she couldn't do it herself. Maybe he was just being polite. Or maybe he was postponing the inevitable goodbye. Levi didn't understand his own motives at this point.

Grace took the blanket she kept in her car for emergencies and wrapped it around the painting. He then placed it snugly between two boxes so it wouldn't rattle around. Finally they were at that moment where Grace had to get behind the wheel. He opened the driver-side door for her, but she paused before slipping inside.

"I'm not sure whether coming to Woodland was such a good idea after all. But I'm glad I got to see you again, Levi. It's...meant a lot to me."

He should have said something short and conclusive at that point. Something like. *Me too. Look us up if you're down this way again. Drive safe.*

But he made the mistake of gazing into her eyes—so large and blue and glazed with tears—and he couldn't look away. And then, as if it had been preprogramed by biology or fate, they were reaching for one another. He cupped one side of her face and slowly brought his lips to meet hers.

He thought she gave a small sob and he pulled back.

"Don't stop," she pleaded. She put her hand behind his head and pulled him back to her.

This deeper kiss made him crazy with wanting her, pushed caution and reason right out of his mind. "Can't you stay," he whispered between kisses, "at least one more night?"

"Is that all you want?"

"Of course not. I wish things were different...that we could have more."

"We could." She pressed her nose against his, something she'd done when they were younger and she wanted him to focus on what she was saying. "I'm only three hours away in Manhattan."

The idea filled him with excitement...but also fear. "What about the Costa Rica trip? And the trip after that?"

"Don't overthink this. One step at a time."

Levi pulled back so he could see her eyes. It amazed him that this beautiful, accomplished woman could really want a small-town man like himself. But if he went...what if he disappointed her? And then there was his daughter. This definitely wasn't the time to start a long-distance affair.

"I wish I was the sort of man who could head off on adventures with you. But if I was that kind of man, I probably would have joined you in New York when we were both eighteen."

As the glow of hope left her eyes, Grace dropped her arms to her sides. At that same moment he heard a faint chime from his phone in his back pocket—a signal he was getting a text message, probably from his daughter.

And sanity returned.

He brushed her fine hair away from her face and kissed her forehead. He thought of many things he wanted to say to her. Many things he ought to say to her. But in the end, all he managed was, "Drive safe."

And then he let her go.

GRACE BLINKED BACK tears and blew her way through an entire packet of tissues on her way to the interstate. She didn't know if she was crying because of sadness or frustration or anger. Probably it was all three. Plus a whole lot of confusion.

The connection between her and Levi still felt so strong. So why was he so dead set against a relationship? The excuses he gave—his daughter, his store, the fact that they lived in different places—none of them were insurmountable. Couldn't they meet on weekends? Take the occasional trip together?

His daughter wasn't ten—she was almost an adult. Yet Levi seemed to feel he was needed twenty-four seven. Maybe he was. She'd never been a parent, how would she know?

"Enough," she told herself when it came time to merge onto the multi-laned highway. She needed to focus on the road and her driving.

She selected an upbeat jazz playlist from her phone and took a long drink from the water bottle in her cup holder. Leaving would have been much easier if Levi hadn't gone and kissed her at the end like that. Though it wasn't fair to blame just him, since they had sort of melted into one another at the same time.

No, she couldn't blame him for the kiss. But she did blame him for offering her a night of his life, like it was some sort of consolation prize.

Fortunately the weather was good and the traffic was light. She'd been on the road for an hour—one-third of the way home—when Alicia called. Her phone was connected with Bluetooth, but Grace let it go through to messages. After a few minutes, she couldn't stop herself from playing the recording.

"*Hey Grace, we're still at the barbecue but we'll be coming home soon. If you haven't left town yet, please don't go. I feel awful about what happened at the barbecue. And you shouldn't be on the road by yourself so late. Please let's...*" At this point the background noise grew so loud Grace couldn't hear the rest of what Alicia had to say. She waited for the click signaling the end of the message and then erased it.

When she got home, she would send a text letting Alicia know she'd arrived safely, but she would wait a few days before calling Alicia back. She was still too hurt, too angry. In a way she could understand Mary Shanahan stepping over the line tonight—she was Levi's mother and obviously would put his interests ahead of Grace's.

But Alicia was supposed to be her best friend. Only, she sure hadn't acted like it tonight.

Another thirty minutes passed. Grace was used to long drives on her own, often at night. But tonight she felt intolerably lonely. She ran though the short list of people she could call at this hour.

Her parents—no, they would sense she was upset and want to know what the problem was.

Alicia—she'd already decided against that.

Which left her landlord Harvey. Hoping he would be home—unlike her, Harvey did have an active social life—Grace made the call.

"How's my favorite tenant?" Harvey said, picking up on the first ring.

"You mean your only tenant? On my way home. So don't panic if you hear noises in my flat later tonight."

"I won't. But if I hear the popping of a cork, I may come

over."

She laughed despite her terrible mood. "That's unlikely to happen. Not much to celebrate."

"You're upset. I can hear it in your voice. Want to talk, sweetheart? I've got my Netflix on hold and a full glass of red."

"It's enough to hear your friendly voice. I've had enough of my hometown and the so-called friends who live there. I wouldn't say I was run out of town. But it sort of feels that way."

"They didn't love your photographs? Your beautiful new book?" Harvey sounded scandalized.

"Oh, they were supportive of my art. What they didn't like was me getting too friendly with my ex-boyfriend."

"Ohhh, this sounds scandalous. Don't tell me. He's married."

"Harvey," she admonished. "You think I'd go after some woman's husband? No, he isn't married. He's widowed."

"So where's the problem then?"

"Exactly. Levi and I are two, consenting, available adults. Yet everyone in town—including my best girlfriend—treated me like I was a praying mantis after the town's most eligible bachelor."

"Is he? The most eligible bachelor?"

"Probably." In her eyes he certainly was. "In the over-thirty category, anyway."

Harvey laughed. "I'm surprised you let those busybodies

push you around, girl."

She thought over Levi's invitation to stay another week, or at least one night. A part of her had been tempted to accept. But Levi had made it very clear he had nothing more to offer.

"Here's the strangest part. Remember me telling you about the grade twelve student who came to Manhattan to interview me?"

"I do. She was the one who suggested you go to the Woodland Autumn Foliage Festival in the first place."

"That girl turned out to be Levi's daughter, Jessica."

"Seriously?"

"Yes. I just figured that out tonight when I saw pictures of her on Levi's fridge."

"Does Levi know his daughter came to see you?"

"He has no idea. But what do you think her motive was?"

"Are you kidding? This is a plot straight from a Disney movie. She was trying to get you and her father back together."

"I wondered if that was it. Only it didn't work."

"Disney plots rarely transfer well to real life. Are you going to call her on it?"

"I don't think so. I'll probably never see Jess…" or Levi "…again."

"You're letting her off easy if you ask me. But you're probably right to move on. Speaking of which, you're welcome to come help me finish this bottle of red when you get home."

"You're the best, Harvey. I may just do that."

"I THOUGHT YOU were staying overnight at your grandparents?" Levi was sitting on the porch when Jess appeared a few minutes after ten. He'd been here since Grace left, mulling over the events of the last week, reliving the intensity of their parting kiss, and generally feeling like he had somehow mucked up his entire life in just seven days.

"Changed my mind." Jess, dressed in jeans and a hoodie, her hair in a ponytail, was standing outside the pool of light cast from the porch, so he couldn't see her face.

"Good. You've been a bit too elusive the past few days. Let's go inside." He pushed himself out of the wicker chair and went to open the door. As Jess walked by he wasn't reassured by her expression. She looked unhappy. And she had dots by her eyes again, a sure sign she'd been crying.

Jess paused in the foyer. She looked through to the kitchen, where two coffee cups and the French press still sat on the table, then to the grouping of paintings, with the obvious blank space where the bluebird had been.

"You've had company. Was it Grace?"

"Yes, Sherlock."

He expected Jess to laugh, or at least smile. But all she

said was, "I heard she left the barbecue early and then you ran after her."

He knew word traveled quickly in Woodland, but this was ridiculous. "Who told you that?"

"Grandma. I don't think she likes Grace much."

Levi studied his daughter's face. She wasn't meeting his eyes—it was almost as if she felt guilty about something. Maybe it was the fact she'd been chatting about him with her grandmother behind his back.

"Grace has gone back to Manhattan, so it doesn't much matter what your grandma thinks of her. Want some hot cocoa and toast?"

He'd started the hot cocoa and toast routine when she was a little girl. Jess had been tracking underweight for her age, and the family doctor had suggested a bedtime snack.

Once the snack was ready they sat at the kitchen table as usual.

"Tell me what's going on," he asked his daughter. "It's not like you to miss a town barbecue. Is it Max?"

Jess's eyes flooded with tears. "I don't want to talk about him right now." She dipped her toast in the cocoa, then set it back on the plate.

Misery came off her in waves and Levi's heart ached for her. "I don't want to pry. I just hate seeing you so sad."

"There's nothing you can do. Max is dating other people, and he doesn't have time for me anymore. It's as simple as that."

Remembering how tight the two of them had been, Levi found this difficult to believe. "That doesn't sound like Max."

"Well I guess he's changed."

"Maybe. But have you tried—"

"Dad." Jess pushed back on her chair so she could stand up. "You can't fix this. Nobody can."

As she ran away, with tears in her eyes, it killed Levi that he was absolutely powerless.

Nov 15, 1999
New York University

Dear Levi,

Yes, I was serious about spending the holidays in New York, but I do understand that you don't want to disappoint your parents. Yes, I'll stick to our original plan, of course I will. I'm dying to see you!

I just realized we hardly texted at all this week. Things are really intense for me right now. I guess it's the same for you. Though Connie did say you hit the party scene pretty hard last weekend. If anything is changing for you...for how you feel about me...you'd tell me, right?

Chapter Twelve

THE NEXT MORNING the sky was full of gloomy, dark clouds that matched Levi's mood perfectly. As he dressed, he listened for the usual signs that his daughter was awake and getting ready for school. But there was nothing. No shower, no footsteps, no closet banging open or closed.

"Jess?" He tapped on her bedroom door. When there was no answer he looked inside. Maybe she'd slept in. But no, she wasn't there.

"Jess?" he called again on his way to the kitchen. He found a note on the table.

Gone for a run. See you tonight.

Levi looked from the note to the threatening clouds outside. It had already started to drizzle. He hoped Jess didn't get soaked. The idea of having breakfast alone didn't appeal, so he decided to go into work early. He took a seat at the counter and waited for Connie to finish handing four coffees in a take-out tray to a young woman he recognized from his bank. He waved to her as she left the store, then turned to Connie.

"Good morning. I didn't see you at the barbecue last

night."

"We were there. But I'm not surprised you didn't see us—there was such a crowd." Connie tucked a strand of her dark hair back into the messy bun on her head. "Congrats on another successful event. Your co-chair sure seemed to be having fun. She was on the dance floor with that new lawyer fella most of the night."

He hoped it was true, that Erin and Oliver were hitting things off.

Connie passed him a mug of coffee. "Want a breakfast sandwich to go with that?"

"Sure, thanks." He watched as she popped a homemade biscuit stuffed with egg, sausage and cheese into the microwave.

"I heard you and Grace left the barbecue early," Connie noted, as she waited for the microwave to beep.

No doubt the entire town knew this. "She needed to get back to Manhattan, so…"

"Well, I was glad to see the two of you reconnecting. I've always felt a little guilty about what happened that first year of college."

"What happened in college…you mean Grace and me breaking up?" There had been no drama associated with it, so Levi didn't understand what Connie meant.

"Um, yeah." Connie's color was high as she plated his sandwich and handed it to him.

"As splits go, ours was civilized. Not to mention over

twenty years ago." Even if it had left him with a broken heart, it had never occurred to him to hold any kind of grudge.

"Right. Of course." Connie seemed flustered, wouldn't meet his eye. "Excuse me, I need to put on another pot of coffee."

Levi watched her for a moment. Did Connie know something about his and Grace's breakup? He couldn't see how that was possible. Not that it mattered after all this time.

He took his breakfast with him to the back office. After all his time away from the store last week there was a backlog of paperwork for him to attend to. But it was hard to concentrate. His thoughts kept drifting, first to Grace, who had texted her safe arrival in New York at ten thirty last night, and then to his daughter, who had to be pretty upset if she'd gotten up early just to run in the rain.

At eleven thirty he left his office to help with the noon hour rush. The first customers he saw were Erin and Oliver. They came through the open entrance holding hands and paused when they spotted him.

"Hey, Levi, sorry you had to leave early last night," Erin said, not looking sorry at all. "It was such a perfect night."

"It really was," Oliver concurred, his eyes, his smile, all for Erin.

How did it happen, Levi wondered, that after months of seeing each other at regular committee meetings, suddenly the two of them seemed totally smitten? Maybe his conversation with Erin had helped clear the air—and let her see what had been right in front of her, all along.

"We're lucky the rain held off until today," Levi said. "Can I help you with anything?"

"We had planned to have a picnic lunch in the park," Erin said. "But we're going to eat in my boardroom now."

"I'll buy us some sandwiches and coffee," Oliver offered. He stepped around Levi and hurried to the lunch counter.

Levi turned back to the mayor. "You look happy."

"I am." Erin stepped closer and lowered her voice. "I thought Oliver was kind of boring and dull, but last night he proved me wrong. Turns out he's an amazing dancer. And we have way more in common than I ever guessed. We've read so many of the same books and we like similar movies and…" She paused and gave a self-deprecating smile. "Sorry. I'm getting carried away."

"Not at all. I'm happy for you, Erin. Happy for both of you."

"What about you and Grace? Are you going to be able to keep seeing one another now that she's gone back to the city?"

"We weren't 'seeing each other,'" Levi corrected. "We're just friends. And I doubt I'll be seeing her again. She's off to Costa Rica soon, on a new project." He forced a broad smile. "Have a nice lunch with Oliver." Then he left before Erin could offer any of her New-Age counsel. If a person's thoughts really did manifest their destiny, his was sure to be dark.

GRACE WOKE WITH a headache, compliments of the bottle of wine she'd shared with Harvey last night. A long shower and two glasses of water helped somewhat. Once she was dressed, she stared glumly out her bedroom window, wondering where all the clouds and rain had come from.

She turned on the TV in the living room, hoping to dispel the cold, sterile feeling of her apartment. The perky man and woman on the network morning show were sharing quips and tidbits of news in a fast-paced and upbeat manner. Grace tried to listen, but her mind felt like mush.

Maybe food—and caffeine—would help. Since all her fridge contained was condiments and a bag of carrots, Grace grabbed her trench coat and umbrella and braved the rain in a dash to her favorite neighborhood café. She told herself she had missed the energy of the city, the quality of the espresso, the texture of the bagels. But the food had no taste in her mouth today. And for the first time it bothered her that she was less than a block from her home and she did not recognize one single face in this café. Even the server and the barista weren't familiar to her.

She finished her latte, ate half the bagel, then put up her umbrella and headed toward Central Park. As she walked she reached to pat her camera case, only to discover she'd forgotten it. Rainy days weren't great for photography, still it wasn't like her to leave home without her camera. She definitely wasn't herself today.

She was walking over the Bow Bridge when her phone rang. Pulling it out, she saw Alicia's name and almost put the phone away again. But she supposed she couldn't put off this conversation forever.

"Hey, Alicia."

"Thank you for answering. I wouldn't blame you if you didn't. I should have been more supportive yesterday and I'm so, so sorry."

Grace let the apology soak in. They were words she had needed to hear. "I wasn't playing games with Levi. I loved him when we were in high school. And…" it was painful to admit, but also necessary "…I still love him."

"I know, Grace, and I'm sorry for not being more empathetic."

"You've got Sean and your kids. When you come to visit me in the city, you see a lot of fun and glamor. But that's not my normal. I'm alone most of the time. I do have friends, but they're used to me being away for my work. And when I'm away they simply forget about me."

"Well, I don't ever forget about you. I may have been a jerk the last few days but I'm still your best friend. So why don't you come back to stay with us in Woodland and give your relationship with Levi a chance?"

"I appreciate the invite. But I made my feelings to Levi very clear last night. And he basically offered me a week. Nothing more."

"That fool."

Grace smiled. "Thank you for saying that. But I better go. I'm standing in the middle of Central Park in the rain and I'm getting soaked."

With a promise to talk soon, she ended the call and then resumed walking. An hour later she found herself back at her apartment with her thoughts no clearer than they'd been at the beginning of the day.

Last night she hadn't bothered unpacking her car, so she did so now. As she hung Levi's bluebird painting in her powder room—next to the framed collage of the sketches he'd included in his letters, she wondered why she was torturing herself. Just looking at this made her heart ache. But Levi's work was so good—she couldn't hide it away in storage.

Late that afternoon she was trying to decide whether to order in Thai or Indian when Harvey showed up with another bottle of red.

"I've ordered us Vietnamese," he announced, making his way straight to the cabinet where she kept her wineglasses.

"Harvey, you are the best."

"Aren't I though?" He opened the bottle and poured them each a glass. "Now show me your pictures. I want to see this town...and the man who had the nerve to break your heart."

Grace wasn't sure she was ready to look at her pictures yet. But she had to face the images sometime and maybe it would be like pulling off a bandage quick, to do it now. She set her computer on the table and quickly downloaded her memory card.

"I haven't had a chance to edit them," she warned.

"Never mind, let me see them all."

She set up a slide show with a five-second pause, then projected the images to her TV screen. She and Harvey sat on the sofa, sipping wine, and watching as her carefully composed scenes flew by. There were shots of Alicia and her family, shots of the town and the park and Levi's store, the hike they'd gone on together, and action shots of the festival.

She tried to see it from Harvey's eyes. The small-town charm, the beautiful autumn colors, the sense of community. She hadn't realized at the time how very often Levi was included in her pictures. Even when he wasn't the subject of a photo he could often be seen somewhere in the periphery. If nothing else showed how obsessed she was with him, these photographs certainly did.

"Not too hard to figure out who your guy is," Harvey commented, once they'd run through all the photos. "He's got a Ryan Gosling, everyday man appeal to him. Just looking at his face, you can't help instantly liking him."

"There's that. Plus the fact I took about a thousand pictures of him."

"That was another clue," Harvey agreed. He took a drink of wine, then eyed her speculatively. "Your pictures tell me something else, too."

"Oh?"

"Not only do you love that man, but you love that small town, too."

"That's not true." Something in her balked at the very idea.

"You capture a lot of beauty in your art, but you are not a sentimental photographer. Not normally. Now look at your pictures again."

Harvey made her run the slide show again. And this time, she saw what he meant. The flattering angles, the sweet close-ups, the majestic vistas. There was no evidence of her usual objectivity. It was like she'd been wearing rose-colored glasses the entire time.

And as the awareness built in her, so did the painful hurt of rejection. She was grateful her hometown appreciated her as an artist. But they'd still closed ranks on her, deeming her not good enough for Levi.

She turned off the TV and shut down her computer. "You've made your point."

LEVI LEFT WORK early so he could rake another batch of leaves for his parents, and hopefully grab a minute to talk to his mother. He got his opportunity when she came out with a glass of iced tea.

"You're working so hard, son. Why don't you take a break?"

"Glad to. I was hoping we'd get a chance to talk." He gestured to the wooden chairs by the firepit and waited for his mom to be seated. "I heard you were talking to Grace at the barbecue last night."

His mother lifted her chin defiantly. "I thought that might be what this was about. You can't blame me for trying to protect my son. You'd do the same for Jessie."

"Maybe I'd want to. But I hope I wouldn't. You have no business interfering in my life, especially not behind my back."

"I just want you to be happy. To find someone who will give you the love you deserve. You know her career will always come first for Grace."

"Why are you so intimidated by Grace's success? Are you afraid she'll lure me away from Woodland, and the store, and you and Dad?"

His mother sank back into her chair, wounded. "You make me sound so selfish. But you know you could never be happy living the sort of live that Grace lives."

Her certainty floored him, and he recalled his conversation with Grace, how she'd accused his parents of narrowing his options on purpose. He'd defended them then, but now he wondered. If his parents had left the choice entirely up to him, would he have followed his heart—and Grace—to New York?

He'd never know the answer. And he was okay with that. He'd made a good life for himself and he could never regret any path that had led to his daughter.

"At thirty-eight I'm capable of figuring out for myself what kind of life I want. As for Jessica, I want her to have choices that I never had. So I'm asking you, Mom, get on board with the college plan, okay?"

"But Jessie loves working at the general store!"

"Right now she does. But who knows how she'll think after she graduates college."

"Which is exactly why she shouldn't go. She doesn't even want to."

Levi had never been so frustrated with his mother. He took a deep breath, reminding himself that his mother was only acting this way because she loved them. And she was afraid.

"I'm going to miss Jessie too," he said softly. "But we have to let her fledge the nest. If she comes back after four years, great. If not, that'll be great, too, because she'll be doing what makes her happy."

His mother scowled at him. "I don't like it. But I see your point." She sighed and then her features sank with regret. "Did we ruin your life, your father and me, by expecting you to take over the store?"

"No way. I'm not saying that. I'm just asking you to

trust me—and my daughter—to make our own decisions."

"Are you—thinking of making changes?"

He could see the worry in her furrowed brow and hear it in her voice. With his father's new health issues, no doubt she was feeling vulnerable. "Whatever choices I make, I'll always be there for you and Dad. You don't have to worry about that."

WHEN LEVI GOT home, he was disappointed Jessie wasn't back from school yet. He checked his phone and saw that she was going to be at cross-country training for another hour. He'd bought an unbaked lasagna from the store, so he turned on the oven. While waiting for it to heat, he paced the house, unable to relax.

It was fine for him to be all noble and talk about Jess being free to make her own choices. But what was his own life going to look like once she was gone? What if she did decide to live somewhere else after graduation? Was he prepared for that?

Jessica was growing up, but instead of embracing the opportunity for a new stage in his life, he was retreating into the shell of the old. Woodland, the store, his parents. It was a life that had been perfect when he was raising his daughter.

But what about the future? He'd lashed out at Grace when she invited him to Costa Rica. Could it be that he'd simply been afraid? With Jess out of the nest, he now had the opportunity to make bolder choices for himself than he had when he was a young man. If he was brave enough.

He went to Jess's room and stood at the doorway. She still had her favorite stories from childhood on her bookshelf. *The Giving Tree* and *Charlotte's Web* right next to the *Three Dark Crowns* series. On her desk were the trophies she'd won at track and field and cross-country, while a huge bulletin board over her desk held pictures of her friends, ticket stubs from plays and concerts, the postcards his parents had sent her while on their RV adventures.

The room was like a time capsule of the first eighteen years of Jessica's life, during which he'd played the starring role as her father. He would be relegated to supporting actor in the next eighteen years, and that—as he'd made such a point of explaining to his mother—was as it should be.

A chime from the kitchen signaled the oven had reached the required three hundred and fifty degrees. He was about to go put the lasagna inside, when he saw something strangely familiar. He turned back to his daughter's desk.

A faded old shoebox was sitting next to her trophies, under a stack of books. The brand name was from a store that had been out of business for at least ten years. He slid the box out from under the books and checked the labeling on the side. *Men's Size 10.*

This had been his shoebox, and he could picture exactly the shoes that had once been inside. Black, leather brogues he'd bought for his senior graduation. He'd replaced the soles two times on those shoes before he'd finally thrown them out. But the box he'd used for something else.

Letters. Grace's letters.

Slowly he removed the lid. And there they were. A stack of letters, the top one with his first-year address written in Grace's hand. But why did Jess have them? He took a closer look at the books that had been on top of the box and then realized what must have happened.

When she was digging through the attic for the year-books, she'd found these letters. Come to think of it, that was also the day she'd asked him if he had any old girl-friends.

He picked up the box and carried it out to the kitchen. After putting the lasagna into the oven, he sat down and pulled out all the letters.

He couldn't remember whether it was his idea or Grace's to send each other letters by snail mail when they could already communicate by phone and messaging. Grace had wanted him to include sketches in his letters. And he'd just liked the idea of holding a piece of paper in his hands that had recently been touched by her.

Corny and old-fashioned. But oh how excited he'd been on the days when a letter from her came in the mail.

At first they'd exchanged letters at least every week. As time passed and their workloads grew heavier, a bit more time passed between them. Until that awful day when Grace had written to him suggesting they be free to see other people.

He'd written a response that he'd never mailed, and he found it now at the very bottom of the stack. Still sealed. So that was one letter, at least, that his daughter hadn't read.

Grace hadn't sent any more letters after that, and neither had he. Just thinking back on that time made Levi sorrowful. He pushed the letters aside and went to the fridge to grab salad fixings. He paused before the door, as dots began connecting in his mind.

Grace's fascination with his fridge art—in particular the photos of his daughter.

Jess's trip to New York, a mere week before Grace herself turned up in Woodland.

And, of course, the box of Grace's letters on Jess's desk.

JESS HAD PUT off going home for as long as she could. But at ten minutes past seven—their usual dinnertime—she finally trudged home from the library where she'd been going through the motions of studying.

She understood that her dad was worried about her. But talking about Max wasn't going to solve anything. In fact, it only made her feel worse.

"Sorry I'm a bit late," she called out as she hung up her jacket and removed her shoes. She set her backpack on a chair, then went to the kitchen sink to wash her hands.

The rich scents of Italian meat sauce and melted cheese hung in the air. In normal times her mouth would be watering. Her dad was already sitting at the table, where he'd placed a huge bowl of salad. She looked around for signs of the main course, then realized it was still in the oven.

She peeked inside and saw one of the awesome lasagnas they sold at the store, the top deliciously browned and bubbling. "Is this ready? Should I pull it out?"

Realizing he hadn't said a word since she came in, she turned to her dad. His hands were folded on the table and his eyes—which were trained on her—seemed sad and disappointed. She glanced back at the table. She'd seen something that didn't belong...

And then she spotted the shoebox.

Oh no. Why hadn't she put that back in the attic? At first she'd been too lazy. Then too preoccupied with what was going on with Max.

"Dinner will keep," her dad said, his tone frighteningly serious. "Let's talk about this first." He pushed the box of letters to the forefront.

Jess hung back, leaning against the counter. The ache she'd been carrying inside herself for days now was suddenly a caldron of anxiety. She couldn't remember seeing her dad like this before, so serious and disappointed.

"I'm sorry for looking at your letters. But I didn't read the...private parts."

"They were all private parts. But let's leave your trespassing on my privacy to the side for now. What did you do after reading these letters? Please tell me you didn't contact Grace. That you—my daughter—are not the reason she decided to come to the Woodland Autumn Foliage Festival this year."

"I—may have been." She felt like she'd drunk a potion that had made her ten inches tall. She dropped her gaze to the floorboards and added, "Actually, I'm sure I was."

"That trip you and Max made to New York...?"

She felt an extra pang, remembering how supportive Max had been, even though he'd been—wisely it turned out—against her plan. That had been one of the last times she could remember things being normal and good between the two of them.

But now she had even more problems to worry about, and these were all her fault. "I arranged to interview Grace. I told her it was for a school project on women who rose to the top of their careers."

"And was that true?"

"Not really. Though I did do a report on her latest book for my American literature class."

"Why did you do it, Jess? What did you want from Grace?"

"This is going to sound stupid. I thought it seemed like you and Grace had a real connection. And I guess I hoped that if I could get her back to Woodland, the two of you would meet up again and, maybe, fall in love."

Her father stared at her. Dumb stricken.

"It didn't take me long to see it was a stupid plan. Grandma told me how Grace broke your heart when you were in college. And then I realized I was just setting you up to be hurt again. And it happened, didn't it? She was here and everything was wonderful and now she's gone and you're alone again... I really am sorry, Dad."

Her father shook his head slowly, as if in disbelief that his own daughter could sink so low. "I hope you understand what it is you should be sorry for. The condition of my heart and whether or not I feel alone isn't it."

She swallowed hard, but her throat still felt dry.

"You should be sorry you read my letters. Sorry you lied to me about your reasons for going to New York. Sorry for arranging a meeting with Grace under false pretenses. Those are the things you should be sorry for." There was a moment's silence, then he added, "I still can't believe you did any of those things. To say I'm disappointed is a real understatement."

Tears began leaking from the corners of her eyes. This time she forced herself to look directly at her dad. "It was all my idea. Max tried to talk me out of it. He only came along to New York because he didn't want me traveling alone."

"That shows some sense on Max's part."

Her tears were now streaming down her cheeks. She'd thought she'd felt miserable before but letting down her dad was the worst. "What can I do to make this right?"

"You need to confess everything to Grace and apologize. Not by phone call or email, either. This is something you have to do face-to-face."

It would be humiliating and awful, but Jess could see that he was right. "So...you want me to go back to New York?"

"Yes. Only this time, I'm coming with you."

Nov. 20, 1999
New York University

Dear Levi,

I just got your letter and I'm writing you back right away. I think I understand what you mean about "reading between the lines." Some things are hard to say, especially when you've been friends as long as you and I have. We always knew a long-distance relationship would be hard. Especially with all the temptations and distractions of college life. Maybe it's time we took a step back, agreed to date other people? Tell your mom and dad thanks for the invite, but I'll be staying in New York for the holidays. I have a lot of work to do.

Chapter Thirteen

TORN UP WITH anxiety Grace paced the length of her living room as she waited for Levi and his daughter to arrive Saturday afternoon. In his text message setting up the visit Levi hadn't provided any explanation of its purpose.

Had he changed his mind about the possibility of a relationship between them? Maybe even about coming on the Costa Rica trip? Surely the fact that he wanted her to meet his daughter was a good sign.

That was what Grace hoped during her more optimistic moments.

The more realistic option was that he'd uncovered Jess's deception. But then why come here? Did he somehow blame Grace for being taken in by his daughter?

Grace checked the time. Two more hours to go. Her emails had piled up during the time she'd spent in Woodland, and she had a bunch of post-production work to do on her Woodland photos, but she couldn't focus on either of those right now. She changed out of her forest-green blouse into a dark wine one. Then checked the time again. She hated that one man had the power to turn her into a dithering mess. But that seemed to be the case.

She tried to lose herself in a game of online chess. When that didn't work, she sorted her laundry and threw in a load.

Finally the buzzer announcing a guest at the door sounded. She pressed the code allowing entrance, then opened her door. Looking down the narrow staircase, she spotted Harvey putting on his gloves to go out. The snoop. She'd told him about Levi and Jess's impending visit. He'd probably been watching out his window for their arrival.

"I'm not introducing you to them, Harvey." She crossed her arms over her chest.

"Pardon me? I'm just stepping out to do some shopping."

"Right." She watched as he timed his exit for the exact moment Levi and Jess were stepping in.

"Good afternoon," Harvey said. Once they had passed, he turned to give Grace a wink, before proceeding out to the street.

Joy fluttered inside her as her gaze locked with Levi's. He looked so good in his thick sweater and jeans and tan pull-on boots. So handsome and wholesome and utterly Levi. But the grim set of his mouth, and Jess's obvious trepidation, confirmed Grace's suspicion about the purpose of their visit.

This wasn't going to be fun.

She toned down her smile. "Come on up," she invited, stepping back to make room.

Jess barely made eye contact on her way inside. From her

sheepish demeanor it was clear she'd been busted. When Levi paused at the door, Grace watched him take in her apartment with one long sweeping glance. She wondered what he thought. Her place was so very different than his.

But all he said was, "Thanks for making time to see us."

Did he think there was a chance she wouldn't? "Of course."

"Jess wants to talk to you privately. When she's finished, shoot me a text. I'll be waiting outside."

And then he left.

Stunned by his cool abruptness, she turned to Jess. "Nice to see you again, *Rae*."

Jessica flushed. "I'm sorry I used that fake name. You must have been so mad when Dad told you who I really was."

"He didn't tell me. I figured it out last weekend when I was at your house and saw your photos on the fridge." Grace waved a hand to the cream-colored leather sofa. "So how did your father find out?"

Jess perched on the edge of the sofa, wrapping her arms around her knees. "I stupidly left the box with your letters on my desk. When he saw that, he figured out the rest. Why didn't you say anything to my dad when you recognized my photos on the fridge?"

"I didn't want to be the one to bust you. But I'm awfully curious. Why did you hide your identity from me? And why did want me to come to Woodland?"

"It seems childish now. And foolish. But I was hoping if I could bring you and my dad together, you'd fall in love again. He's been alone ever since my mom died. And I could tell by your letters—even though I only read a few bits of them—that you two had something special."

"That was a long time ago. And those letters were private."

Jess's bottom lip trembled. "I'm sorry I read them. Sorry I lied to you." She dropped her gaze to the floor. "I only wanted to make Dad happy, but instead I've done the absolute opposite. Plus, I disappointed him. And, well, I've disappointed myself too. I should have listened to Max when he tried to talk me out of this."

So the boyfriend hadn't been complicit. Grace had been wondering about that. "It's a hard thing, to admit when we're wrong. So I thank you for doing that, Jessica."

"Can you forgive me?"

"I can and I do. In some ways you did me a favor by inviting me back to my hometown. It was good for me to see the place again. I see it a lot differently now than when I was young."

"Woodland must seem so small and boring now?"

"Actually, the opposite. I was one of those kids who was dying to grow up and travel the world. I don't think I appreciated the beauty of Woodland or the fact that I was lucky to go to high school there." She paused to take a deep breath. "I'm also glad I got to see your dad again. He's a special guy, and you're right, we had a tight bond. Unfortunately, in our case, that bond just wasn't enough."

As Levi paced the block in front of the brownstone where Grace lived, he distracted himself by imagining what it would be like to live here. First he'd have to get used to all the people. Even at two thirty—a quiet time in Woodland with most kids in school and adults working—there was a constant parade. Parents holding the hands of young children, professional types with glazed expressions and Bluetooth earbuds, older folks pushing small shopping carts, and dog owners strolling with their leashed pooches.

He'd have to get used to all the brick and concrete as well. Trees lined the street, but they were surrounded by concrete with only a metal grate to allow moisture inside. Most of the brownstones had been converted to flats that housed at least four if not six families, though there was just one other name posted next to Grace's on her building. Presumably H. Peters was the man who'd been going out when Levi and Jess arrived.

Then there was the noise, mostly traffic but mingled in with the engines and horns he could make out the almost frantic chirping of sparrows. He followed the chatter to a low boxwood hedge that had overgrown its allocated space between the sidewalk and one of the buildings. Levi quickly identified the highly adaptable house sparrow, one of the few species that seemed to thrive in urban settings. He wasn't sure how they did it. There was so little green. Even the dogs in New York had to settle for peeing on concrete rather than grass.

But he shouldn't judge too harshly. He had to admit there was an energy to this place, a vibe that was kind of exciting. And just five blocks away, New York's Central Park was a birder's paradise, especially during migration seasons.

No time for a visit on this trip though.

He glanced up at the second-story windows of Grace's home, wondering what was going on in there. Jess had been so nervous on the train ride to Manhattan. No matter how Grace reacted, it would be a big relief for his daughter to get this over with.

As for Grace, he could only imagine what she thought of his daughter's scheme. Or his parenting abilities, for that matter.

His phone chimed and he pulled it out of his back pocket to read a message from Jess.

All done. Grace wants to talk to you.

Be right there, he responded.

He hurried up the walkway, feeling apprehensive. Grace had good reason to be upset, but he hoped she hadn't been too hard on Jess. He was about to press the bell to gain admittance, when the gentleman from before stepped past him.

"I can let you inside. You're Levi Shanahan I presume?"

Levi nodded, making room for the well-dressed, older man to unlock the door. "And you're H. Peters?"

"Call me Harvey. This is my home. I've been renting the upper apartment to Grace for about five years." He inserted the key into the lock then turned back to Levi. "You're Grace's bird nerd friend from Woodland. Must say, you don't look the part."

This man must be a friend as well as a landlord, if he was in Grace's confidence. "You thought I'd be wearing a khaki vest and a Tilley hat with field binoculars strung around my neck?"

Harvey chuckled. "Something like that." With the door open he made an elegant hand motion for Levi to precede him.

As he climbed the stairs, Levi sensed the older man watching him. When he turned to look, however, the foyer was empty.

When Grace opened the door, Levi felt a burst of pleasure at seeing her again, even under these circumstances. His gaze dropped to her lips as he remembered their last kiss...

"Hey, Dad." Jess gave him a wan smile from her seat on a spotless, cream-colored sofa.

He looked her over. "No blood. Things went okay?"

Grace smiled. "We've sorted things out. Jess tells me you're planning to head straight home. Want a coffee first?"

He met her gaze for a few seconds as he recalled the last

time they'd seen each other, on the night he'd tried, unsuccessfully, to stop her from·leaving Woodland. "Thanks, that would be good."

"Great. It's already made. Black, right?"

As she turned to the kitchen, he took a closer look at her home. They were in a long room with a waist-high bookshelf separating the living area from the kitchen and dining table. The walls were neutral, the furniture modern and understated, leaving the art—large, colorful abstract pieces—to take central stage.

"You don't have any of your work on display," he noted. "No photographic art at all." And no sign of his little watercolor either. He felt embarrassed he'd even given it to her. The quality just didn't compare with what she already owned.

"That's business. I like to buy art from the places I visit and especially from artists I've actually met." She handed him a cup of black coffee. "Sit down. Relax."

He had never felt less relaxed in his life. But there were things that needed to be said. He glanced at his daughter. "Would you mind giving me a few minutes alone with Grace?"

Jess jumped to her feet. "Would I mind having some free time to roam around Manhattan? You're kidding, right? Can I have an hour?"

"How about thirty minutes? I'll meet you outside at—" he consulted his watch "—quarter after three."

"Got it." Jess turned to Grace. "Thanks again for being so nice about this."

"No problem. Just—be your honest self from now on, okay?"

"I've learned my lesson. I promise."

Once Jess was gone, Levi set down his coffee. "I need to apologize for my kid. I had no idea what she was up to. She's never pulled a scam like this before. I guess I trusted her more than I should have."

"Don't be so hard on yourself. She's almost eighteen. You can't have the control over her that you had."

"Yeah, that was my thinking when I okayed the trip to New York." He went to the window and looked out to the street he'd been pacing a few minutes ago. He was a man who was used to being decisive, who knew his place in the world. But the past few weeks had changed him, and so many emotions were churning inside him.

"I never should have kept those letters," he muttered.

"I'm not sorry you did."

He turned from the window to her. In all probability this was the last time he would see her. Which made this the only opportunity to ask her something he'd always wondered. "Grace, when you wrote to me suggesting we see other people...was there already another guy in your life?"

She folded her arms over her chest and tilted her head. "Of course not." She hesitated. "Is that what you thought?"

"Why else would you have suggested we see other people?"

"Because I knew you wanted to be free." She ran her hands up and down the silky fabric on her arms. For the first time that afternoon, she'd lost her air of composure.

"What made you think that?" he asked quietly.

"Connie told me."

Levi blinked. "You've lost me. What does Connie have to do with anything?"

"Connie and I kept in touch during first semester of college, though we drifted apart soon after the Christmas break. She told me that you had met someone but that you were too honorable to do the long-distance breakup thing. She warned me that you were probably going to do it over the Thanksgiving holiday."

"That doesn't make sense. Connie knew how much I was looking forward to seeing you over the break." By then Grace's parents had already moved to Florida, but Grace had agreed to come to Woodland and spend Thanksgiving with him and his family. He'd had every minute of their four days together mapped out.

"You weren't already in love with Maggie?"

"I didn't even meet her until six months later." Which meant Connie had been lying. "Why would Connie want to stir up trouble between you and me?"

Grace raised her eyebrows. "Maybe so she could make a move on you?"

Oh man. He'd been so blind. He sank into a chair near

the window and shook his head.

"I thought she was my friend." Grace looked sad and troubled. "Did the two of you ever…?"

"No. Definitely not." Now Connie's earlier comment about him and Grace, the guilty flush on her cheeks, made more sense. Anger flared, but only briefly. What good would come from blaming Connie for something she'd done twenty-odd years ago? Her life, like his, had not been easy.

"You know what I hoped would happen after I sent that letter?" She blinked back tears. "I hoped you'd take the first possible train to Manhattan and tell me that you didn't want to see other people. That you only wanted me."

"The idea didn't occur to me," Levi admitted. "Our lives were already on a different trajectory. I think a part of me had already accepted we wouldn't last. I just hadn't seen it coming that soon."

GRACE WRAPPED HER arms around her waist and stared out the window, his words repeating in her ears:

Our lives were already on a different trajectory. I think a part of me had already accepted we wouldn't last.

She wanted to stamp her feet. To scream. To shake him. "You talk about our different paths, as if that were the only thing that mattered. What about our feelings? That sense of rightness when we're together?"

"I don't deny I felt those things back then." He hesitated.

"And I still do. But—"

"Stop." She put her hands over her ears. She'd wanted to stay calm and in control today, but it simply wasn't possible. "I don't want to listen to you recite all your reasons we can't be together again. It's just garbage, Levi. But you don't see that. You'll never see it."

His face took on a hard, grim look. "So my life in Woodland is garbage? Thanks for clarifying that for me."

Oh, he was impossible. "That is not what I meant."

"I'm sorry our small town isn't good enough for you. I happen to love it. And I think it's about time I got back to it."

"If you want to purposefully misunderstand me, then go ahead." She went to her door and opened it. And when he left without another word, she was almost glad. Five minutes later she was crying. Fifteen minutes later she was angry again.

And then, with perfect timing, she heard a knock on her door. For a wild moment she hoped Levi was back, this time to apologize on his own behalf. But of course it was Harvey, with a nice bottle of Cab Sav.

"Don't look so disappointed," Harvey said. "From the stormy look on your man's face, he's going to take a day or more to calm down."

"He's not my man. But I accept your gift of wine. Do we have to wait for five o'clock?"

"On this occasion we bend the rules." Harvey took the

bottle to her kitchen where he opened it and poured two glasses.

She accepted the glass when he passed it to her. "Cheers." She took her first drink. "That helps." She went to the washroom to blow her nose and rinse her face. While she was there, she took a moment to appreciate the new bluebird painting. Yes it was beautiful. But maybe it was time she redecorated and finally put her high school romance in the past where it belonged.

When she returned she said, "I look terrible."

"After a fashion. Your terrible is not like most people's. You have this unflappable quality that is very disarming."

"It's a ruse. I feel very flapped right now." She sank into the sofa with her glass of wine. When Harvey started to speak, she raised her free hand to stop him. "Say anything right now except that you liked the look of him."

Harvey kept his mouth shut.

"I knew it," she muttered. That was the problem wasn't it? She was furious at Levi right now, but she still couldn't help loving him, and what was almost worse, liking him.

"Tell me what happened," Harvey said.

She didn't think she wanted to talk about it, but once she started, she couldn't stop. She told Harvey about Jess's apology, how it had been sincere and heartfelt, then about Levi and his reaction to finding out that Connie had lied to break them up.

"He made it sound like our love affair was doomed anyway. And I guess it was. Is."

"Are you ready to accept that?"

"What choice do I have? If he can't even take three weeks to come to Costa Rica with me…"

"It's nothing for you to take off on a big trip like that. But for some people a three-week trip to Costa Rica is a big ask," Harvey said gently. "Is it really a deal-breaker for you if he can't go? Have you given any thought to what you'd be willing to give up for him?"

She stared at Harvey, remembering how Levi had accused her of devaluing his life in Woodland. She'd denied the point, but when she looked to Levi to change his life in order to fit in with hers, wasn't that what she was essentially doing? Telegraphing that her career, her life, was more important than his?

"I believe you have a point there, Harvey," she said slowly.

"I usually do."

December 1, 2000
University of Vermont

Dear Grace,

    I'm writing this letter even though I'll never have the nerve to send it. Thanksgiving was so lame without you. I didn't do any of the things I'd planned. Didn't go hiking or birding or play any chess. Went out with Connie and a few other friends one night, but only lasted an hour. You said we should see other people, but it turns out the only person I really want to see is you.

Chapter Fourteen

"I HEARD YOU and your dad went to the city yesterday."

Jess looked over her shoulder as Max ran up beside her. "What are you doing? You hate getting up early." Which was why she'd started running at this time, to avoid him.

"Trying to talk to you." Max adjusted his stride to match hers. "Why are you avoiding me?"

"I'm not." But that was a lie. "I'm confused."

"You're not the only one."

She threw him a questioning glance, but all he said was, "So why the trip to New York?"

"Dad figured out what I did and wanted me to apologize to Grace in person. She was pretty good about it." And Jess felt a lot better now too.

"Did your plan work? Are your dad and Grace—"

"No. All I did was make my dad miserable and disappointed in me."

"I'm sorry about that."

"You warned me. But thanks for not saying you told me so."

"Hey, what are friends for?"

She turned to him, arching her brows. "So we are friends? Lately I've been wondering. Like the night of the bonfire. Why didn't you wait for me?"

He kicked at a stone at the side of the path. "I had stuff on my mind."

Here it was. Max was going to tell her about his new girlfriend. Suddenly short of breath, Jess slowed to a light trot. "Stuff like what?"

"You can't tell anyone else, okay? Not your dad. Especially not your grandmother."

Jess stopped in place. This sounded serious. She focused on Max's worried face. "I won't."

"Dad lost his job last month." Max's shoulders slumped. "Things suck at our house. Mom and Dad fight all the time—though not so much when I'm around."

The problem was his family, not another girl. Jess almost sagged with relief. But then she felt selfish. Being out of work was a big deal for his father, for their entire family. "Is that why you've been going home for dinner? So your parents don't fight?"

"Yeah. Trying to keep the peace. My sisters are being tools...whining because my parents made them drop their horseback lessons. Mom's freaked out because she doesn't think Dad can find another job. And Dad's pissed because he worked twenty years for that company, and now they just downsize and leave him out in the cold."

Poor Max. Stuck in the middle of all his family's unhappiness. "And you? How are you doing?"

"I'm okay." He lowered his head and added quietly, "But if Dad doesn't find work soon, they're going to have to draw down on my college fund."

"What will that mean for you?"

"I figure I'll have to work a year or two before I can start college."

"That's so unfair." Max wanted college so much— definitely more than she did. "I wish you'd told me sooner. I've been so bitchy."

"I shouldn't be telling you now. Dad's paranoid about the whole town finding out. Which is crazy, because you can't keep any secret for long in Woodland."

"Well, thanks for trusting me now."

"Yeah. About that. You know when you asked if I was dating someone?"

Jess nodded, holding her breath.

"I'm not." He reached for her hand. And when she folded her fingers over his, he added, "But I totally want to be."

ON SUNDAY MORNING Levi was packing his lunch when Jess came into the kitchen in baggy flannel pajamas.

"Going hiking?" Jess grabbed a coffee cup and helped herself from the French press.

He gave her a second look. Her voice was bright, and her eyes were glowing. Something good must have happened but he knew better than to ask outright.

"Taking the kayak out to Morley Lake. Want to come?" He issued the invitation automatically though he was really in the mood to be alone. He was relieved when Jess declined.

"Max and I have plans."

Levi stopped stuffing veggies into his pita. His daughter was gazing down into her coffee cup, but there was no hiding the pink bloom on her cheeks. "So the two of you have made up?"

"Yes."

Levi sensed there was more to this. He hadn't seen his daughter so happy in ages. "Fair to say the two of you are dating now?"

She couldn't suppress her smile any longer. "Fair to say."

He gave her a one-armed hug. "That's great news."

"Max and I talked about lots of stuff yesterday. He told me that he needs to spend more time with his family these days. So do you think Grandma and Grandpa would mind if I missed Sunday dinner? Max invited me to his house."

This was different. Max often ate here or at Jess's grandparents, but Jess almost never went to a meal at his house. Levi had always assumed it was because Max's parents had their hands full with his younger twin sisters.

"I'm sure your grandparents will understand." He suspected there was more to this story, but he'd wait until Jess was ready to fill him in. He wrapped up his sandwich and grabbed his water bottle. "I'll probably go straight to your grandparents' when I'm finished kayaking. Should be home by eight."

"I'll try to be back by then too. Have fun."

LEVI WAS AT the far side of the lake when he spotted a male loon dead ahead about twenty yards. He immediately stopped paddling and reached for his binoculars. Common loons were among his very favorite birds. Despite their name, they weren't always easy to find. The birds were shy of people and noise and they didn't live in flocks like many other aquatic birds such as gulls and ducks.

He focused in on the bird, so handsome with his sleek black head, black and white collar and checkerboard body. Spotting a loon was always a thrill, but even better was hearing them call out to one another with their hauntingly beautiful wail. Levi tucked his paddle inside the boat and sat back, prepared to wait and see if he would get lucky.

There was plenty of nature to appreciate while he sat here. The sugar maples had lost their bright red leaves during last week's rain, but there was still lots of gold and orange foliage compliments of the oaks and beeches. Mirror images of the trees and the blue sky were perfectly reflected in the calm lake.

Levi reached for his sandwich, and munched away slowly. During moments like these, thoughts and worries from his regular life generally fell away, and he was filled with an inner peacefulness and wonder, that he should be so lucky to live in such a beautiful world.

But today he could not stop thinking about Grace. He thought about her home in New York, the frisson of excitement he'd felt as he'd imagined living in such a place. He pictured her getting ready for her trip to Costa Rica, and all the amazing experiences she would have when she got there.

The way he had felt when he kissed her.

The deep sadness in her eyes when he pulled away…

He'd told her their lives were on different trajectories, and that had been true. But a trajectory could be altered by a change in force.

As a young adult he'd repressed the call to adventure which Grace had embodied. He'd said no to his love of art, and travel, and allowed his choices to be shaped by the expectations of his parents and his community.

Grace had blamed his parents for that.

But it had been what he wanted. He'd taken the safe route, and it had given him twenty good years. What about the next twenty, though? He had to give his daughter credit for recognizing that it would take something explosive to shake him out of his complacency.

Not that he condoned what she'd done.

But it had been effective.

His daughter leaving for college wasn't just about her life…it also signaled a new stage for him. It was up to him what he did with it. If he did nothing, from this point onward he would always wonder what if…

What if he'd gone to Costa Rica?

And, more importantly, what if he'd told Grace he still loved her?

A haunting wail floated over the calm surface of the lake. *Where are you? Where are you?*

The male loon raised his head and stretched out his long neck.

The call came again. *Where are you? Where are you?*

Suddenly the loon began flapping his wings furiously. As his heavy body rose out of the water, he began using his webbed feet to run along the water's surface, using both wings and feet to propel him faster and faster until finally he was able to gain the speed for liftoff.

Levi watched as the male flew out of sight, presumably toward his mate on the other side of the lake. For another minute he sat, contemplating what he'd seen.

Then he picked up his paddle. It was time to go home.

DINNER AT LEVI'S parents always followed a leisurely rhythm. A game of cribbage with his father in the back sunroom, then carving the Sunday beef roast for his mother while she made gravy. Usually Jess set the table, but in her absence, Levi's dad stepped in.

"So Jess and Max are an item now?" Levi's mother asked.

"Looks that way," Levi confirmed.

"I'm happy for Jess. She's liked Max a long time," his mom said. "But it doesn't feel like Sunday dinner without her."

Levi's father grunted his agreement. "Wonder if his father has been impacted by the layoffs at Ameri Plastics?"

Levi looked at his dad. "I never thought to ask." This could explain the changes in Max lately. Levi felt ashamed that he'd been so preoccupied with his own life he hadn't thought to take Max aside and ask if everything was okay.

Once they were seated at the table, their plates full, his mother said, "It's nice having life back to normal isn't it? Seems like every year the crowds for the Foliage Festival get bigger and bigger. I understand it's great for our economy. But I'm always relieved when it's over."

"Are you going to co-chair the committee with Erin again next year?" Levi's father asked. "She's quite the woman our mayor."

"Yes she is, and no I'm not," Levi said. "I'm planning to scale back my volunteer work for a while."

"But is that wise? With Jess going to college, you'll have extra time," his mother pointed out.

"Yes." Then, wanting to plant the seeds for the changes he hoped to make in his own life, he added, "I was thinking

I'd like to travel."

"You still have the store," his father reminded him.

"I have a good staff and assistant manager. Plus, I happen to know the former owner." Levi gave his dad a wink. "I know your diagnosis means you have to slow down. But how would you feel about checking in on the store now and then for me?"

His dad chuckled. "I'd love it. If your mother lets me."

"Just how much are you planning to travel?" his mother asked, sounding suspicious.

"That will depend on a few things. I'll get back to you on that next week."

His parents exchanged looks. Levi could tell they wanted to ask questions. His mother even opened her mouth.

"Will you—" she began. Then she glanced again at his father and started again. "Will you pass the potatoes please?"

WHEN LEVI GOT home after dinner with his folks, Jess was waiting for him and in the mood to chat. It was great to see her happy again, and when he mentioned the layoffs at Ameri Plastics, she admitted Max's father had been let go.

"But they aren't telling anyone, at least not yet."

"I won't spread the news," Levi promised her. "How is Max feeling about all this?"

"It's hard. Money is a problem. Max may not be able to

afford to go to college this fall."

"That's rough, I'm sorry. Tell Max, if he needs a part-time job now or a full-time one in the summer, to come see me after school tomorrow."

"Thanks, Dad. I was hoping you'd say that."

They chatted for a few more minutes, then after Jess went to her room, Levi took a cup of coffee out to the porch. He loved the air on these late autumn nights, the musty-sweet scent from the decaying leaves, tinged with woodsmoke from neighboring fireplaces and bonfires.

He wanted to talk to Grace. To tell her he regretted the things he'd said to her on Saturday. And to share the epiphany he'd had out on the lake on Sunday.

But it didn't seem like the sort of conversation that could be held over the phone. He'd have to take another day off work this week and drive up to see her.

The next morning he called her from the breakfast table, hoping to make a plan.

"I've been doing a lot of self-examination. I need to talk to you. Could I come to the city and take you to lunch tomorrow?"

"That wouldn't be a good idea."

He was silenced by an overwhelming sense of loss. He slumped back into his chair and wondered what to say. A few awkward seconds went by.

Finally she spoke. "You don't need to go to the city because I'm on my way to Woodland."

Could it be? He straightened his spine and looked out the kitchen window, as if her Audi might drive into view any second. "That's great. How far away are you?"

"Over an hour. I'll come to the store when I get there."

THE GORGEOUS RED, yellow and orange foliage had dulled since Grace's last visit, but as she drove past the *Welcome to Woodland* sign, she had to admit the town still looked pretty. She found a parking space across from the general store and took a moment to collect her thoughts.

Then she grabbed the small cedar box from the passenger seat next to her and got out of her car.

Warm scents of apple cider, pumpkin pie and coffee greeted her as she went through the store's open front door. At least a dozen customers were milling around the place and several were lined up at the till.

Grace was surprised to see Levi at the register. He was so focused on his customer he didn't notice her, but she took a moment to enjoy watching him. She loved the way he focused on other people when he was talking to them. Levi truly cared; it wasn't an act.

She shot a brief glance to the back of the store where the lunch counter was. Most of the stools were occupied, blocking any potential views of Connie. Just as well.

She joined the queue at the checkout. Soon there were

just two people ahead of her. Then one.

And finally Levi saw her. She watched as a smile appeared on his face and grew and grew. She moved up to him and set the cedar box on the conveyer belt.

"Can I help you, miss?" A teasing light glinted in his gray eyes as he stared at her.

She basked in the warmth of his full attention. Something fundamental had changed in him. He'd lowered his barriers. She could feel the energy building and snapping between them.

"Your daughter told me you saved my letters. I wanted you to know, I saved all my letters from you, too." She opened the box then and revealed her stash. The letters she'd read and reread so very often in that first year of college. Eventually she'd weaned herself off the letters, but not to the point she could throw them away.

But the other night, after Harvey's comment, she'd read them again. And recognizing the pure love that Levi had poured into them she wondered why she'd believed in Connie's lie so easily? Maybe she'd been too young at eighteen to commit fully to one man, even a man as wonderful as Levi.

She wasn't sure that was true. After so many years she could only guess.

But she did know how she felt now. And she needed to make sure Levi understood before they walked away from each other for a second time.

Levi looked down at the letters, then back into her eyes. "So I wasn't the only sentimental one."

"No."

He covered her hands with his for a moment, then turned to the customer behind her.

"I'm sorry, sir, I have to go now but someone else will help you." He waved to a young man stocking the candy shelves. "Justin, please take over for me."

Then he hurried out from behind the counter and took Grace's hand. He led her to the back of the store, to the chess table in the private corner behind the potbelly stove.

"There's so much I need to say to you. I'm not sure where to start."

"Is this about our different paths?" she asked warily.

"Not at all. I've been doing a lot of soul searching since I saw you in New York. I finally realized that when I say I can't go to Costa Rica with you because of my obligations, I'm just using them as an excuse. I'm in a rut because it makes me feel safe and comfortable. I lost my wife just a few years after losing you and I guess I created a nice, safe world for myself trying to protect myself from another loss."

"Maggie was so young when she died. I can see how traumatic that must have been."

"It was. But it was also twenty years ago. And when I think of the future and all its possibilities, I feel like I'm ready to soar again. If you'll still have me, I'd love to go to Costa Rica with you."

"I'll still have you." Grace could feel the tears forming in her eyes.

"Good," Levi said. "Because the moment I saw you in the pet food aisle of this store, I knew you still held a piece of my heart, that you always had, and you always would."

Grace was overwhelmed. She'd come here today with hopes, but she'd also been afraid to hope for too much. She brushed away her tears with the back of her hand, then mustered a smile. "Just a piece?"

"As it happens, my entire heart is currently available."

Grace leaned forward until the tip of her nose touched his. "So is mine," she whispered. "And now you have to let me say my piece. When I look at the life you've created for you and your daughter here in Woodland, I see something beautiful and rich and true. You give so much to other people. Not just to your family, but to the entire community. I don't want to be the person who changes your world. I just want to expand it a little. Enough to include me."

"Does that mean you would not be averse to spending more time in Woodland? Maybe make it your home base between travels?"

"You are my home base, Levi. If you're in Woodland, then I want to be in Woodland."

Gently Levi touched his lips to hers and pulled her closer. Grace forgot entirely where they were; she lost track of how much time had passed. Not until Levi stopped kissing her and gave her a smile, did she notice that a bunch of people—both staff and customers—had gathered around the potbelly stove. They were smiling and clapping and—would you look at that—Connie was at the very forefront of the group.

Postcard from Los Cusingos Bird Sanctuary
November 14, 2019

Dear Jessica,

Grace and I are having a terrific time. I can't wait to show you all the photos when we get home. Hope things are going well at school and the store and with Max. Look forward to seeing you soon, kid.

Love, Dad

Epilogue

Thanksgiving, 2019

AS LEVI PULLED his truck in front of his parents' house, Grace's stomach tightened with apprehension. What kind of welcome was she going to get after taking their son thousands of miles away for three weeks…especially after they broke the news that after Christmas they were going back for another three weeks?

"Costa Rica blew my mind," Levi said. "But I sure am excited to see everyone. I hope Jess and Max are here already."

Grace smiled at him. He looked so handsome and healthy with his tanned skin and gold-streaked hair. They'd landed at La Guardia last night, slept a solid, if short six hours at her place in Manhattan, then hopped into his truck first thing in the morning. She understood his excitement to see his family again. But she sure had loved having him to herself for three weeks.

Levi reached over to squeeze her hand. "I can't wait to tell them our news."

"Me too." She just wished she could be as sure as he was

that their news would be greeted with happiness.

As she stepped out of the truck, her boot sank into six inches of snow, compliments of a low-pressure system that had moved into Upper New York state last night. Grace marveled how a town that had been vibrant with greens and reds and golds just one month ago was now a crisp and clean winter wonderland.

Levi grabbed the bag of gifts they'd brought from Costa Rica, then took her arm. "Careful not to slip." He pointed out two sets of footprints already leading up the path to the front door.

"This must mean Jess and Max are already here," he said.

And at that moment the front door opened, and Max and Jess appeared, both with shovels in their hands.

"Dad!" Jess dropped her shovel and ran to her father. As they embraced in a tight hug, Grace smiled at Max. "Happy Thanksgiving, Max."

"Same to you. We were hoping to get this path cleared before you arrived."

"It sure came down, didn't it?" As Grace started plowing her way toward the house, Jess came up and wrapped an arm around her shoulder. And then there were three of them, Grace, Jess and Levi, linked into a chain.

"Did you have a good trip?" Jess asked. "We can't wait to see your pictures."

"And I can't wait to hear your news," Levi said. "I want updates on school, the store, everything."

They'd tried to stay in touch on their trip, but their remote destinations hadn't made it possible.

"Everything is fine, Dad. You're not as indispensable as you thought," Jess teased. She gave him another hug. "But it sure is nice to see you."

In the front foyer everyone removed boots and coats. Delicious aromas of home-baked bread, roasting turkey and pumpkin pie lured them into the kitchen where Pat was peeling potatoes and Mary was stirring cranberry sauce on the stove.

"Did you finish shoveling already?" Pat looked up and then broke into a grin. "Mary, they're here!" He dropped his peeler and went to hug his son. Grace was surprised and pleased when he hugged her next.

"Hey, Dad, Mom. Happy Thanksgiving." Levi wrapped his arms around his mother and lifted her right up from the floor.

Mary laughed, then patted his check and turned to Grace. "So you brought him back."

"Always," Grace replied.

A slow smile warmed Mary's face. She patted Grace's shoulder. "I can't remember when I saw my son looking this happy."

Later Grace realized it was in that moment that she felt fully accepted by Levi's family. Acceptance was cemented when she was asked to help set the table and then later, allowed to help wash the dishes. She wasn't being treated as a guest but as a member of the family.

During dinner Jess told everyone that Max had good news to share. With help from the school guidance counselor, he'd applied for a bunch of bursaries and scholarships and had ended up being successful in covering the cost of tuition for next year. That money, plus his earnings at the general store, meant he would be able to attend college in the fall.

"Not the University of Colorado, as I'd planned," Max allowed. "But I hear University of Vermont has some good things going for it, too."

"Good things like me." Jess's smile couldn't have been happier.

"Speaking of good news…" Levi reached under the table to take Grace's hand. "We have some of our own. Grace and I have decided to get married."

There were excited gasps, followed by happy congratulations. Everyone seemed genuinely pleased. Finally it was Jess who asked the burning question.

"Where will you live?"

Grace turned to Levi, her best friend, her first lover, the man she wanted to spend the rest of her life with. She would let him answer this one.

"The plan is for me to join Grace on her travels when I can. It won't be all the time. It may not even be fifty percent of the time. But as much as possible."

"Levi made a bunch of beautiful sketches in Costa Rica

that I'll be including in my next book. So hopefully he'll keep doing that, as well," Grace said. "And between trips, when I'm doing post-production work or writing my books, I'll live with Levi here in Woodland."

"Dad, your life needed some shaking up. I think this sounds awesome."

"Well, you started the shaking, that's for sure," Levi said.

When Levi, Grace, Jess and Max broke out laughing, Levi's parents turned to him for an explanation.

"What does Jess have to do with you and Grace finding each other again?" Mary asked.

"I'll let Jess tell the story," Levi said.

When all eyes turned to his daughter, she took a deep breath. "It all started in the attic…with an old shoebox of Dad's that was full of love letters…from Grace."

THE END

Want more from C.J.? Check out *A Cowboy's Proposal*, book 1 in her Shannon Sisters series!

Join Tule Publishing's newsletter for more great reads and weekly deals!

More books by C.J. Carmichael

The Shannon Sisters series

Book 1: *A Cowboy's Proposal*

Book 2: *A Convenient Christmas Proposal*

Book 3: *A Hometown Proposal*

The Carrigans of the Circle C series

Book 1: *Promise Me, Cowboy*

Book 2: *Good Together*

Book 3: *Close to Her Heart*

Book 4: *Snowbound in Montana*

Book 5: *A Cowgirl's Christmas*

Book 6: *A Bramble House Christmas*

Bitter Root Mysteries series

Book 1: *Bitter Roots*

Book 2: *Bitter Truth*

Book 3: *Bitter End*

Book 4: *Bittersweet*

Available now at your favorite online retailer!

About the Author

USA Today Bestselling author C. J. Carmichael has written over 50 novels with more than three million copies in print. She has been nominated for the *RT Bookclub's* Career Achievement in Romantic Suspense award, and is a three time nominee for the *Romance Writers of America* RITA Award.

Thank you for reading

Letters From Grace

If you enjoyed this book, you can find more from all our great authors at TulePublishing.com, or from your favorite online retailer.

TULE
PUBLISHING